Sweet Tea for Frankenstein

ANNIVERSARY EDITION

JILL LOPEZ

Em Dash Press

ISBN: 978-0-578-27488-1

Book cover design by Amy St. Clair.

Printed by Em Dash Press, LLC in the United States of America.

First printing 2010.
Anniversary edition 2022.

Em Dash Press
TheEmDashPress.com

For my family.
Some by blood and some by water just as thick:
Thank you for your golden light.

Chapter 1

Tuesdays are my favorite days. That's because every Tuesday night I babysit with my best friend Rachel at our church. And I use the term "babysit" loosely because there are rarely any babies involved. We're only there in case someone needs us to entertain a younger sibling during the program for the grade-school kids. So we have an official excuse to hang out and also do some homework, and those are the best nights—the nights where we get a little giddy and test the limits of the church nursery cribs to see if they can hold our weight (they can't). And to further misuse church property, this crisp mid-September Tuesday I decided to experiment on our most cherished toy in the entire nursery: the chatter phone. It is vintage and fabulous.

I plucked the phone from its resting place on the middle shelf of the nursery's gigantic wall of toys and unwound the magenta pull string. Rachel, eyes glinting, watched from her perch on the rocking chair with the

Noah's-Ark-patterned cushions. I pliéd to the floor and secured the pull string to my ankle with a tidy double knot. Standing back up, I squared my shoulders and lifted my chin like an Olympic gymnast preparing for her gold-medal routine.

I took off running, spanning the entire length of the room in four strides, then turned back around to run the other way. The phone obediently trailed after me, emitting the gurgling, spastic rings and chirps that Rachel and I have come to love. The two mechanical blue eyes on the front of the phone swiveled up and down in time with its launch across the nursery floor, as if the phone itself were rolling its eyes at me, but maybe loving every minute of it just the same.

Rachel's laughter echoed off the walls, and she was doubled over in the chair as I ran laps around the room. Without warning, the side door opened and who should waltz in but Mrs. Thomas, Travis's mom. Travis, of course, is the "lucky" guy I've had a huge crush on since I was ten. *Panic.* Of all the people.

I dove into the rocking chair beside Rachel, struggling to tuck my string-tied ankle under me and sweep the phone under the chair and out of sight. The phone was having none of it, and protested in mini-chatters. Rachel and I might not be the most mature thirteen-year-olds we know, but we're absolutely the most fun.

Mrs. Thomas took us in with the steady gaze of a mother who immediately knew we were up to no good.

Her eyes flicked to the chatter phone as she made her way across the room. "Just passing through." She opened the door on the other side. "You girls play nice."

I caught her smile as she closed the door behind her.

Rachel and I turned to each other, mortified, before laughing so hard we had to concentrate to breathe.

"You should've seen your face!" Rachel shrieked.

"Oh no." I pulled my sweater hood down so it covered my face. "Do you think she'll tell my dad?"

Rachel rolled out of her chair and collapsed into a heap on the floor, her fist pounding the carpet. Gradually the giggles died away, and she turned to me. "What was your experiment, anyway?"

"To see if I could wear out the phone, or if it would wear me out first." I kicked my foot out in front of me so the phone hung suspended in air, staring at me, with its painted red smile upside-down.

"The smart money's on the phone, without a doubt."

I nodded miserably. "True story."

Rachel caught my eye, stifled a laugh as she muttered "You girls play nice!" and that set us off again.

A few minutes later when my parents walked in, Rachel and I were ready with our security measure firmly in place. We've trained ourselves to know the exact time the children's program wraps up, and were prepared with our math books open. When my parents opened the door we were putting on our best studying show ever, in case word of my phone experiment had already reached my dad's ears.

We shouldn't have bothered with the act. One glance at their faces told me they had been crying, and they didn't even notice Rachel was in the room. Confusion trickled through my veins. Was this related to me running around with a toy phone, or what?

Dad's tired, chocolate eyes settled on me, his mouth a tight line. He took a deep breath. "Annie, remember that doctor appointment we took Daniel to yesterday?"

Ok, I guess we were getting right to it. I felt my head nod obediently—my brain instantly relieved that my little brother Daniel was the cause of worry this time—and tried not to notice as fresh tears blazed a mascara trail down my mom's face. There had been several appointments lately, and more than one hushed phone call with my mom's voice shimmering with worry as it floated out of her bedroom.

Dad continued. "They just had us come back in. They're saying Daniel has a brain tumor."

"A *tumor*?"

The words burst from me like staccato bullets, shooting through the air and rendering my mom unable to stand without Dad's arm to hold her up. And there I was, faced with their grim, devastated presence, just wearing a surprised grimace and swallowing a lot. My mind raced: *A brain tumor?*

I felt acutely aware of the *plick-plick-plick* of the clock.

The sniffles. Rachel lightly gasping "Oh, no," from a place that sounded far away. Maybe I was supposed to burst into tears, to wring my hands and fall to the floor. But all I felt was shocked and awkward, as if my own tumor-free brain had suddenly turned to mush.

I finally came up with words. "But what does that mean? Will he need surgery?" Had my hands always felt this bulky and strange?

Dad cleared his throat, which made Rachel jump just a little. "He might. We can talk more about it at home."

My feet shuffled themselves forward and I offered a stunned, robotic hug. "Wow. I'm sorry."

Dad looked over at our math book props. He noticed Rachel and her horrified expression, and gave her a little nod. "I'll give you some time to pack up. Come find us when you're ready to go."

And then they were gone. Staggering through the same doorway Mrs. Thomas had disappeared through mere minutes earlier, like it was all a bizarre dream. The *click* of the door closing echoed in my ears as I felt my eyes flick over to Rachel.

She closed the distance between us and squeezed my shoulder. "That was crazy. Are you okay?"

A slow sigh failed to deflate the balloon of pressure in my chest. "I don't know, honestly. I don't know what I expected, but it definitely wasn't a brain tumor."

She nodded sympathetically and glanced down as her

phone buzzed. "Oh man, that's my mom. Do you need me to stay? You look…not great."

I laughed and gave her a feeble shove. "Nah, you go. I'll text you later."

After a quick hug and a sad, backward glance, Rachel was gone. Alone in the quiet, I lowered myself into the rocking chair and thought about how this had all begun.

We knew something was up with my ten-year-old brother Daniel ever since our family vacation the summer before. It was my big sister Tracy who actually made the discovery. She and Daniel were playing volleyball and I was off somewhere, probably reading as usual. As Tracy told the story, she was serving to Daniel and noticed he always flailed wildly and missed the ball when she served it to his left. After that, she and my parents flooded him with their own tests.

Like one time, they had him hop around on first his right foot, then his left; and then touch his thumb to each finger on first his right hand, then his left. It *did* look like something weird was going on and maybe he wasn't faking it for the attention. Whenever he did something involving his left foot or hand, the movements seemed imprecise and difficult. My dad's friend said they should take Daniel to see a neurologist. At the time I didn't think much of it besides feeling a little annoyed that once again Daniel was the center of attention, and I was pushed to the background. Surely he was fine, I had thought. But I was wrong.

Daniel had a brain tumor. For real. Now what?

I felt my thoughts begin to fuzz at the edges. Suddenly feeling exhausted, I hoisted myself out of the rocking chair and made my way out of the nursery to find my parents.

There were still a lot of people around. The children's program had ended at least thirty minutes ago, and the parents picking them up don't usually tend to linger.

Tonight was different. I could feel the electricity in the air as I headed into the sanctuary and the sound of conversation. There was a group of rowdy third-graders running around on the stage at the front, oblivious to the human drama that was unfolding elsewhere in the room. Usually Daniel was running around too, but I didn't see him anywhere. I spotted my parents, engulfed in the circle of several parishioners whose heads were shaking slowly from side to side, pained expressions on their faces. Dad talked animatedly and Mom stood there looking numb. Some people had their hands over their mouths, and I watched someone place a reassuring hand on my mom. The sentiment was kind, but it didn't register. I could see that much from all the way across the room. She was in an unreachable place.

I should probably mention at this point that my dad is the pastor of our church. That's right, I am a dreaded "PK," which stands for "pastor's kid" and all the angst that goes along with it. You see, I have this theory. And the theory is that pastors' kids can pretty much only end up one of two ways: You can end up a total rebel, or you can try hard to appear perfect. And you know what? I think there's remarkably little difference between these two types, because they're both a mask to protect who you really are against those all-seeing eyes that expect you to never screw up and then pounce when you do. Because I deeply desire to stay off the radar, I choose the goody-goody path. All of us Spencer kids do, it's easier that way. Plus, I wouldn't want people thinking bad things about my parents because their kid acts out.

The thing about the miss perfect act, though, is it's tough to keep it up. I do everything I can to keep up appearances: I help my mom teach Sunday school, I help with nursery duties on Tuesday nights with Rachel and am on the rotation for Sunday mornings too, and I act sweet and smile and speak politely with everyone. You'd think that would be enough, but it never is. It always feels like every little thing I do or say gets noticed. Wearing mismatched socks (it was an accident, I swear!), sneezing too loudly, an ill-fated and unsuccessful flirting attempt with Travis. You name it, I've been called out for it.

And now it was happening again. I heard my name being spoken somewhere and my eyes immediately found the source. It was Mrs. Diaz. I felt myself relax a little. Dawn Diaz is the nicest person ever. She's the type who always goes out of her way to give me hugs and relay her own middle child horror stories whenever she senses I need it. If you're unfamiliar with the struggles of being a middle child, consider yourself lucky. My older sister

Tracy can already drive, and she's always been the "in charge" responsible one—even when she was my age. Daniel is super smart and always gets the "Aww, you're so cute!" routine and special treatment. But nobody knows quite what to do with me. It's like I'm too young and too old at the same time.

Mrs. Diaz caught my eye and waved me over to the grief circle. "You poor thing," she crooned, crushing me in a hug that felt more intense than usual.

I smiled a sad smile. My inner world was still too big a mess to come up with anything coherent that would contribute to the conversation. Besides, what could I say? I probably didn't know any more about what was going on than she did. Mrs. Diaz echoed my sad smile, then slowly turned her attention back to my mom.

I became aware of myself standing outside of the circle that tightly held my parents like some kind of protective wall. Where was my wall? I wanted a wall. More than that, I wanted to go home.

After a few attempts to peer through the cracks in the people wall and catch my dad's eye, I succeeded. Unfortunately, once he noticed me, everyone else did too. I heard some low murmuring, and someone nearby reached out to squeeze my hand.

"We'll sure be praying for your family," someone else said, but it all felt like a blur of faces.

I mumbled "Thank you" as I nodded, my eyes to the ground. Now the protective wall was *facing* me! That was way more overwhelming. After a few more hugs and exchanges, my parents mercifully headed out the front door.

"Where's Daniel?" I asked.

Mom nodded at Mrs. Thomas as we passed her on our way to the parking lot. "He's home with Tracy. We dropped him off after the appointment instead of dragging him here with everybody finding out about his tumor."

Well. At least Daniel had avoided the firing squad for now.

The drive home was heavy with silent questions. Was I supposed to ask them out loud? Should I ask what was going to happen next, or would it be better to wait until we were all together? Part of me was bursting with all of the confusion and what-ifs, but a bigger part knew it was best to stay quiet for now. They looked so tired.

My phone lit up with a text from Rachel, a question mark that I answered with a shrug emoji.

I don't know anything yet, I wrote. *Talk tomorrow?*

Ok, she texted back. *My mom said to tell you she's so sorry about this, and that you're welcome to crash at our house whenever you need.*

I texted back a blue heart emoji. Good old Rachel.

Chapter 2

My family has lived in Chandler, Arizona ever since I was three years old. Our house is the only home I can remember, and I've always loved it. It definitely has at least five different colors of carpet going on, and it isn't fancy or anything, but when you walk in the front door it feels warm and you can tell a family lives here.

When my parents and I arrived home from church that night, I wasn't greeted by that feeling. I felt something new and uncomfortable. Daniel had a brain tumor. I immediately sought out Tracy, the mother hen, my heroic big sister who always listens to me. Would she understand how weird I felt about all this?

I heard her voice coming from Daniel's room, so I peeked around the corner and saw that she and Daniel were in the middle of a game of Monopoly. "Come on out and face my hotel row. You can't hide in jail forever," Tracy sang.

Daniel scowled. "Watch me!"

Tracy turned and saw me leaning in the doorway. "Good, you're home. Can you believe this is happening?" She sighed so deeply it seemed to come from the tips of her aqua-painted toes.

I bit my lip, not trusting my voice. I bet Tracy was the first person my parents told. Clearly she was reacting to this news exactly like you'd expect a big sister to, and I felt an irrational jealousy that her feelings were uncomplicated and appropriate. But Tracy is almost seventeen years old, plus in a lot of ways she and I have super different personalities. She's outgoing and fun, with a life packed full of friends and cross-country track and a choir she's in at school that gets to travel around sometimes. She has her own job as a server in a restaurant, and even has a car. There's so much of her life that happens outside the walls of our home, so much more she can reach out and grab when things here go sideways, like they're doing now.

I, on the other hand, am a much quieter person who would rather have a few good friends and not a lot going on at once. I love to dance, but other than that, it's hard for me to express myself sometimes. What goes on at home is a much bigger part of my life than Tracy's, too. Whenever things are frustrating at home, it bleeds over to color my whole world with broad strokes of gray.

Tracy's gaze was so intense it was unbearable, and my eyes instead chose to inspect the contents of Daniel's floor. Discarded clothes, his baseball glove, and an assortment of toy cars lay strewn across it. And there was Tracy and Daniel's Monopoly game, mid-slaughter, hotels and Chance cards spilling out of the tattered box as if it were any other night.

My heart jolted a little. I *couldn't* believe this was happening, but I also highly doubted anybody else in the family felt quite like I did, unable to express much sympathy because part of me screamed in frustration. Daniel already got so much attention, and he would get even more now. Unbelievable. But as the dark feelings swirled in my heart, a blade of shame pierced through. What kind of sister gets jealous of her brother's brain tumor, anyway? It's not like he chose it.

My gaze darted from Daniel's eyes to Tracy's, twin sets of Mom's vibrant, expectant blue quite different from my own brown eyes that I get from Dad, but I said nothing.

Speak, Annie!

I could see the remnants of tears on Tracy's face. "This game is definitely over," she said, getting up to leave. "Go on, he won't bite," she muttered in my ear, nudging me into Daniel's room and closing the door behind her.

Her words, though gentle, stung at my brain like a colony of wasps. What was I supposed to do? I glanced down and saw my math book still under my arm, a freshly scrawled "Annie + Travis" on the brown grocery bag I'd made into a book cover. Had I written that only tonight? It seemed like forever ago.

I shifted the math book to my other arm. "How are you feeling?"

Daniel shrugged and scratched at a bug bite on his arm. We did not have a super touchy-feely relationship, and this already felt awkward. "Same as I always feel."

"That's good."

See? He wasn't acting any different than usual, why should I? Maybe I should've been able to hug Daniel and cry like Tracy could, but even under these circumstances that felt like it would be unnatural for us both.

I settled on saying "Well, I guess I'll say goodnight. I'm sorry about your busted head."

He laughed and crossed his eyes.

I backed up and banged into the wall with a muffled *thud* instead of finding the doorknob.

"Who has the busted head?" Daniel said, giggling his little-boy giggle.

Why was I afraid to give Daniel a hug? Did I think he was going to spontaneously combust?

"Hey kids, let's all have a talk." Dad's strained voice floated down the hall. We all obediently piled into the living room and sat down more or less in a circle.

"What's going to happen?" asked Tracy, impatient to cut to the chase.

Dad took a deep breath and regurgitated news he'd likely already told twenty church people. "Tomorrow we'll take Daniel to the hospital so they can run more tests and figure out what to do. They are admitting Daniel for at least a few days because there are a lot of things to consider about treating his tumor. They need to find out the exact dimensions and location of it, and whether it's cancerous or not. We might be heading toward chemotherapy or they might be able to remove it with surgery."

I'd gulped at "cancerous" and flinched at "surgery," glancing at Daniel. He looked small sitting there, just a kid minding his own business, growing a tumor. I looked over at Mom and could practically hear her brain running through every worst-case scenario. Her eyes were fixed on a point in the middle distance, a definitive line sharp between her eyebrows. She gripped a mug but didn't drink from it. Dad sat forward in his chair, elbows on knees and hands folded. Eyes toward the ground. It was hard to see my parents like this. My dad has always been a solid, nurturing presence in our home. He has a way of understanding people, and is dedicated to helping them— especially all the people at our church. My mom possesses a quiet strength that shows up whenever someone in our family or church has a need, expressed or otherwise. Calm and capable, Mom always knows how to solve a problem. Except now, they looked like they were each trapped in their own echo chamber of haunted thoughts.

Dad cleared his throat. "There's not much more we know at this point. It will most likely be a few weeks of being at the hospital a lot. We will all need to pitch in, and lots of people at church are offering to help with meals and transportation. It's going to be tough, but we'll make it through."

Tracy's eyes were sharp and concerned as she took in their faces. "Is there anything we can do?"

Dad raised his eyes. "Always. Let's pray for Daniel."

We all grabbed hands and Dad's voice rose, clear and strong. "Dear God, we come to You with faith knowing that You hold this situation in Your hands. We know You love us and have a perfect plan for each one of us. We pray for Daniel to be healed completely, and for You to guide his doctors' hands. We pray You would give our family peace and comfort as we all go through this. Amen."

We all murmured our own "Amen" and I felt like an imposter sitting there with a thorn of distrust in my heart. Why would God let this happen to us? What had we done wrong? We were a family who served Him. Even so, I added my own silent, selfish prayer, that I wouldn't disappear in the storm that was coming. I looked around guiltily, wondering if anybody else could read my thoughts. But nobody was paying attention to me. Mom and Dad were gazing at Daniel, Mom with her hand resting on the back of Daniel's chair. Tracy sat cross-legged on the couch, picking agitatedly at a fingernail. She was looking from Dad to Mom and back again with mingled frustration and resignation, like she had about a million more questions but knew they probably didn't have the answers. Daniel himself sat slouched in his chair, eyes fixed on Dad, his legs swinging back and forth through the chair legs. Did he realize how serious this was? Maybe it was better if he didn't.

As for me, I didn't know what to ask. My experience with tumors and cancer was limited to what I'd seen on shows and movies, and second-hand information from when Rachel's grandmother had battled and ultimately beat breast cancer a few years back. Nothing prepared me for what to expect when a *kid* had a tumor, and in his brain, of all places. Besides, the *real* questions I had deep down, I couldn't ask and they couldn't answer. Would Daniel be okay? What was the worst that could happen? How would all of this change our family? I realized I hadn't said anything the entire time our family sat there. I hoped they would all understand that it was because I was lost in my own thoughts, and not that I didn't care.

I barely slept that night, but I doubt I was the only one. I was trying to pinpoint exactly what it was I felt. Was it guilt? Maybe. Guilt because I couldn't muster up tears of anguish about Daniel to prove I was a human being. Everything would be okay. Right? *Sigh.* I couldn't even gather the strength to journal about any of this. And for me, that's really saying something.

I heard a soft *meow* as Smokey, our grey-and-black-striped cat, jumped up onto my bed.

I whispered into his warm, downy fur. "You like me best, don't you?"

Smokey stared at me in response before deciding to climb onto my pillow and settle on it in a furry heap. Not a lot of manners, that cat. Maybe he forgets what he owes us.

We've had Smokey since he was a teeny kitten, with eyes barely open yet. Some people from church had found him under their backyard shed and called us. Everybody knows my mom is the person you want in your corner when there's any kind of pity-case cat involved. She's a very nurturing type of person that way. They may as well fashion some kind of bat signal for her: *We found some scrawny kittens! Please help!*

Anyway, Smokey's mom had been moving her whole litter of kittens when a dog scared her off in the middle of her efforts. They didn't know how long Smokey had been alone out there under the shed, but when we took him home he wasn't much more than a pitiful, skinny thing the size of a hamster.

This all happened more than three years ago, but I'll never forget what those first few days with Smokey were like. Mom recruited me as her nurse assistant, and the two of us took turns feeding Smokey from a special kitten bottle every few hours. We sat up some nights just cradling his tiny body, warming him in our hands, searching for any sign he was going to be okay. And there were times when we didn't know if he'd make it, but he really pulled through. Like I said, my mom's the one you want taking care of stuff like that.

I scooted my head to the bottom corner of my pillow

as Smokey took sprawling liberties with the rest of it. He probably still thinks he's the teeny kitten who used to curl up to sleep right in the crook of my neck. Smokey always purrs me to sleep, and I like to think he's guarding me. It reminds me of all those nights Mom and I spent worrying over him, and I figure he wants to return the favor.

Even with Smokey there, I slipped in and out of fitful dreams about the chatter phone, huge and loud, chasing me down a dark hospital corridor. In the dream I hurtled toward a glowing *Exit* sign, but there was no door.

Chapter 3

The next day at school I expected everything to be instantly transformed by the tumor news, like at home. I was greeted by brilliant, tedious normalcy. Hallelujah. It's always nice to be at school where at least I have more freedom to be myself. Nobody is looking at me as the pastor's daughter or Tracy's little sister—or now, the sister of the little boy with the brain tumor. I felt light and free, with only a small, dark corner of my heart pulsing with the knowledge that Daniel was heading to the hospital later today to have more tests done. I knew there was only so long I could avoid thinking about it, but now was not the time.

At lunch, Rachel was waiting for me at our usual table outside. I noticed the rest of our lunch crew was nowhere to be found.

"I thought, I mean, in case you wanted to talk alone or something," she said.

Normally lunch is a pretty rowdy affair, with five of us

girls crammed around a table and trying to talk over each other to be heard. There's usually Rachel and me, Katie, Liz, and Shannon. I'm not as close with the other girls as I am with Rachel, but I'd wanted their noisy company today to drown out my thoughts. Too bad it was just the two of us as far as the eye could see, and off in the distance, was that a lonely tumbleweed scuttling by?

I sat down next to her. "Sorry I didn't text you back."

She shrugged. "I knew I'd corner you eventually and get you to spill the beans."

Rachel and I grew up together since her family started coming to our church when she was only five years old. And since we live close to each other, last year Rachel and I began seventh grade at the same junior high. It was nice to already have a built-in friend like her. And this year, it makes life feel a little more settled to know we have math together to look forward to every day (well, as much as you can look forward to math class).

Rachel and I talk about everything. She complains about how boring it is to be an only child, and I remind her that having a pretty track star for an older sister and a smart, angelic little brother is no picnic, either. When she groans about having to hide candy and eat vegetables all the time because her dad manages a health foods store, I complain that being the pastor's kid is a frustrating lot in life due to constant pressure to be perfect. We go back and forth this way, but I guess the tumor news tips the scale my way for most pitiful life situation. Lucky me.

I automatically held out my hand. "Peeps."

"Oh, come on," Rachel whined. "These are the only ones left from last year's Halloween batch."

I cleared my throat, and looked Rachel squarely in her green eyes. "Ma'am, I require Peeps."

Rachel growled at me and dug into her backpack. *Score!*

"Now that's more like it, Rach."

She handed over four extremely stale pumpkin-shaped Peeps.

Peeps are what every marshmallow wants to be when it grows up—jammed into festive shapes and covered in colored sprinkles. They're like junior high currency around here if you didn't know, and it is an actual art form to get them to just the right state of staleness.

I took a big bite and pretended to drool on Rachel. "Mmm...lost in Peep-land..."

"Don't be gross. You have orange sugar all over your face now." Rachel laughed as she tried to brush some off of my chin.

I swatted her hand away. "Thanks, mom, next time please spit on a napkin first, so as to achieve the full effect."

Rachel rolled her eyes. "Okay, tell me, I'm dying to know what's going on." She shifted to be directly in front of me and my sugary face. I froze mid-Peep.

"There's not much to tell right now. My parents and Daniel are going to the hospital after school today, and they're going to run a bunch of tests. He's going to stay there for a few days while they figure out whether to do chemo, or it could be surgery."

She leaned back in her blue plastic chair. "Sucks either way, I bet." She waited for me to say more, but all at once I felt the full effects of my terrible night of sleep and could only grunt in reply. "And how are you feeling about all of this?"

Didn't she need to have a couch handy if she was going to make me talk about my feelings? I looked away and cleared my throat. All the joy of my stale Peep evaporated. "I don't know. Pretty shocked still. Can't really picture what's going to happen next. Can we please talk about something else right now?" I sounded more impatient than I meant to. So much for school being a place untouched by the tumor cloud.

She sat back and held up her hands in mock surrender. "All right, all right. No need to be such a jerl about it."

Despite my dark mood, I laughed. "You just said *jerl*! What the heck is a *jerl*?"

She pondered this a moment. "I did, didn't I? I think I was trying to say jerk and girl, and it came out jerl."

"I like it. Like if someone is being a jerk in a girly way, or something."

She beamed, and I had successfully distracted my best friend. She started talking about something funny that had happened in her Spanish class, and I relaxed. She is such a good friend and she knows me better than anyone. Still, for some reason I didn't feel like processing all of my family drama with her right now.

Chapter 4

When I got home from school that day, things already felt different than they had the night before. It was like the family was moving on to some sort of phase two. As if by magic, the lethargic grief of the previous night had been swept away by an urgent busyness. And wouldn't you know, as I walked home from school I had just started to feel legitimately and entirely sad about everything that was happening. I had clearly missed my chance. Everyone was too busy rushing around preparing for the coming days to notice I had finally achieved an appropriate reaction. As usual, I was a little behind.

Mom was like a Tasmanian devil in the house, whipped up in a furious flurry of activity. I saw her just long enough to notice she had replaced her usual friendly pastor's wife face with a different kind of face. This new face had a mouth clamped tight as if to stifle a scream. It had eyes set with intensity and singleness of purpose and a little bit of fear. But I don't think I was supposed to see the fear part.

Dad's face was set more gently than Mom's, but I could tell he was trying to be part of the action, too. There went Mom down the hall getting Daniel's MRI pictures ready to go to the hospital. There went Tracy into Daniel's room to pack some things for his hospital stay. There danced Daniel looking less scared than amused.

And there paced Dad. "Should I grab Daniel's toothbrush or anything?" he called down the hallway.

Tracy's voice answered from Daniel's room. "I got it already."

Dad caught my gaze and raised both eyebrows at me. He already seemed a little older than he had on Monday.

It didn't seem like there was any meaningful way I could contribute, I just felt like I was in the way. So I slipped down the hallway and into my room, opened my closet door and pushed the hanging clothes aside, and went in. There's a small hollow place behind my clothes where the long dresses and old dance costumes form a curtain that could completely conceal me from outside eyes. My secret space. I reached up in the dark until I felt the cord, and turned on the desk lamp that's clipped to a small bookcase I also managed to squeeze into the closet. The bookcase of course serves the function of housing my favorite books, along with my pen collection. I only collect pens of remarkable design and quality. These aren't just any pens.

I know, pretty babyish for a thirteen-and-a-half-year-old to have to hide in the closet, but I think everyone needs a place to go that's all theirs. And it's not like I would sit in my closet all day long like some weird hermit creating a fire hazard and being all crazy about pens, I just needed to feel more protected sometimes, that's all. And this was one of those times.

I could still hear Mom and Tracy scurrying up and down the hall, but I doubted they realized I wasn't around. And if they did notice, I'll bet they thought I was better off out of the way.

Angry thoughts crept in, about being outside of it all, left out and forgotten like I always was. I felt my pulse thunder in my temples, and the warm prick of tears stung my eyes. For the first time, I allowed myself to actually think about what the coming days would be like, and the story played out in my imagination like one of those frilly, overly sobby movies. You know the type, like: *Brave Family Endures Shocking Illness of Family Favorite.*

I sighed and hugged my knees up to my chest, feeling the tears slide down one after the other. Family favorite. I think Rachel coined that term for Daniel because she'd witnessed more than one occasion when I'd been blamed for picking on him and I didn't do anything wrong in the first place. And even if I did do something wrong, I'll tell you this: it's tough not to want to pick fights with a little brother your parents hug and stare at with twinkles in their eyes. Especially when there you sit, and you're not the cuddling age anymore but secretly deep down you wish you were. Rachel understands that and she's an only child.

I could feel my face hardening into a brooding scowl, when an image of Daniel's face flashed across my brain. Breezy, happy, carefree Daniel, whose entire mouth would end up stained purple every summer from devouring endless popsicles. The poor kid. I felt a hot stab of guilt that my first reaction to this whole tumor business hadn't been overwhelming concern for him. What was the matter with me? After all, annoying family favorite or not, he was my brother!

He was my brother, and I was Annie. Quiet and not especially remarkable, but someone afraid of ending up outside of it all, the kid left over who nobody knew quite what to do with.

The rest of the week inched by. I went to school, going through the motions of attending classes, laughing with my friends, and avoiding Rachel's probing glances.

It was quiet at home now. My mom and Daniel had practically moved into the hospital for the rest of the week, with her looking resolute enough to set up camp in Daniel's hospital room and remove that tumor herself if the doctors would let her. Daniel had been pouting because they wouldn't let him bring his Legos to the hospital. And Dad had placed one hand on top of Daniel's head as they'd all rushed out the door, and even though his eyes weren't closed I knew he was praying.

There wasn't much cause for Tracy and me to go with them at first, so we stayed home and enjoyed a few afternoons of freedom. Tracy had told her boss about what was going on, and she'd been given the rest of the week off. It was nice, just Tracy and me. On Thursday we did our homework at the kitchen table before lounging around the living room, eating ice cream right from the carton, and watching true crime documentaries until Dad came home and made us go to bed. Smokey took his normal spot on the furthest arm of the leftmost couch in the room. He was close enough to bask in the glow of the television and the warmth of our laughter, but far enough away to have a good head start if he sensed he was about to be scooped up and cuddled.

I tried not to think about what was going on at the hospital, like maybe it was better not to know anything than to know too much. I think Tracy and I had a silent agreement to pretend, if only until we heard otherwise, that nothing was wrong.

Dad shattered our silent denial Friday night by arriving with the latest news. He still had all his regular responsibilities at church, but went straight over to the hospital whenever he could.

He set down his laptop case and sat on the arm of the couch while Tracy paused the TV. "Here's what's up. The doctors have finished running all the tests on Daniel. They want to go over the results with us tomorrow morning and talk about a plan of attack. Mom and I thought you both should be there, too."

Tracy and I looked at each other. I felt a hot coal of dread sink into my stomach as a shiver raised goosebumps on my arms. It was really happening.

"How's Daniel doing? How's Mom?" Tracy turned off the TV and started to collect our scattered dinner dishes from the coffee table.

Dad did a half-smile and slowly moved his head from side to side in a gesture that said *Oh, you know.* "They're trying to make the best of it. Daniel is his usual self, not scared or asking a lot of questions. Mom is trying to be patient and trust the process. It's been tough not knowing what we're in for. It'll be good to have some answers."

I nodded and helped Tracy with the dishes. There was no going back now. Like it or not, this train was in motion and we were all along for the ride.

Chapter 5

Bright and early the next morning we all ate a morose breakfast of cold cereal before climbing into the car. We rode in tense silence to the hospital, Tracy drumming her fingers on her knee the entire time. When we got there, we hurried across the parking lot—Tracy and I jogging to keep up with Dad. We followed him through the broad metal double doors to a small side room where Mom was already waiting.

"Daniel's resting in his room," she said, reaching over to squeeze Tracy's hand and giving me a weak smile. She looked pale and exhausted, her eyes puffy. Dad handed her some coffee he'd brought from home, and squeezed her shoulder.

We all sat in the waiting area for a few minutes before a tall man in scrubs and a white overcoat showed up.

He shook Mom's and Dad's hands, then escorted us into his office. "I'm Dr. Gill, I'm a neurosurgeon here," the man said to Tracy and me. I was momentarily distracted by the strong impression that Dr. Gill actually looked like a fish. I know that's maybe mean, but seeing him up close with his bulging eyes and pale, green-tinted skin, the resemblance was uncanny. Only after this thought passed did I register how he'd said he was a neurosurgeon. So, it was going to be surgery, then? My heart started to gallop. Surgery seemed so much more violent than chemo.

We each took a seat in Dr. Gill's office—Mom busy pretending not to study the degrees on the wall, Dad's eyes skimming the bookshelf, and Tracy and me by the door, just quiet.

Dr. Gill was carrying some charts and several MRI scans. He set the charts onto his desk and situated two of the scans into a glowing rectangle on the nearest wall. He sat down heavily in the black leather swivel chair behind his desk and got right to it. "From these images we can tell Daniel's tumor is a benign pilocytic astrocytoma with an accompanying cyst. The tumor's the size of a golf ball, and it's all situated right in the middle of his right hemisphere, in his speech and language area."

He pointed out varying angles of the tumor and cyst on several MRI images, including one that showed which parts of Daniel's brain were in charge of what function. He switched them out for other scans and explained how they had injected Daniel with a special dye that only reacted to cancerous cells. There it all was in shocking, glowing black and white—blobby foreign objects surrounded by glowing brain matter. I couldn't make sense of it, but none of it looked good.

"So what does that all mean for Daniel?" asked Mom.

Dr. Gill leaned forward in his chair. "Well, the fact it's not cancerous is great news. We want to treat it surgically, but due to the location and size of the tumor and cyst, it'll be a long and difficult surgery. Plus, there are some risks we're taking by operating on a tumor located in that area. Daniel could lose his ability to speak, or could lose his ability to understand words altogether."

I saw Mom shrink into her chair. I could almost see the heartbreaking scene playing out in her head. Daniel staring at her blankly while she tried to make him understand "I love you."

But Dr. Gill kept right on going. "And of course with a surgery this intricate there is always the risk for paralysis or something more serious. We need to be prepared for every possible outcome." Dodging my parents' wide-eyed gazes, he cleared his throat and picked up one of the charts.

I heard a heavy sigh come from Dad's corner of the room. "There's no reason for us not to expect everything will be fine, right? This will be a long and difficult surgery, but Daniel could come out of it just fine?"

"Of course," Dr. Gill answered, as if that part wasn't as important as the terrible things that could happen instead.

Or he could come out a vegetable, I couldn't help but think. What would that be like, for Daniel not to understand what we were saying? This was all so weird, so wrong. Because Daniel is smart. He's so smart that my parents always show off his skills to their friends like he's some genius. But now? What if he couldn't talk? What if Daniel could never walk again?

I glanced at Tracy out of the corner of my eye and saw a tear slide down her cheek. I reached out to hold her hand, and she squeezed mine back. Slowly, confusion and worry crept their misty tendrils into my thoughts. Daniel was only ten, so he'd be okay, right?

Chapter 6

When Sunday morning came and it was time for church, I dreaded going. I expected things would be like they were on Tuesday night, only on a larger scale, and I was right.

I got "the look" wherever I went—you know, like the half-guilty look of people who were definitely talking about you before you walked within earshot. Most people were still in the stage of finding out about Daniel's tumor. It was weirdly funny, you could see it spread like a ripple effect—only the ripple was people talking about us and that didn't feel good.

I looked out across the sea of condolences and saw Travis looking straight at me and giving me a half-smile. Nodding hello, but not coming closer. Normally I would've taken this as a sign he was definitely about to propose to me. But today I was seeing everything and everyone in a whole new light. Travis and I had known each other for most of our lives, but really, were we even friends? How much did he understand or care about what was going on?

There was a strangeness all around me that I hadn't felt here before. Even Mrs. Diaz only gave me a little wave from across the crowded foyer before scurrying away when I saw her before the service began. Usually she comes up to me on Sunday mornings to give me a big hug, asking "How's my favorite middle kid?" But the look on her face today was more like she was thinking I was glass that could break right before her eyes. Or maybe people thought it was all contagious. The sadness, the shock, the family member with a tumor, all of it.

Why was it that while so many people from the church said they were pulling for our family, I had never felt so isolated? I wondered what Tracy felt. All I knew was that members of the congregation—people who had always been like family to me—now shot furtive looks at me with something like pity in their eyes.

I tried to find Dad, but he was of course surrounded by many church members speaking earnestly in low voices. One look told me to stay away.

Luckily, Rachel was there. Just when I felt tempted to run out of the building, she quietly steered me to our usual seats toward the back of the sanctuary, kindly deflecting some of the looks that came my way.

When the service began, I thought maybe the worst of the day was over. I was wrong. As soon as Dad stepped up to the podium to give his sermon, I could tell we were in for some heavy seas. His eyes were still wild and reeling with disbelief from the news we'd gotten the day before. He looked unsteady, like he was about to fall over and was clinging to the podium for support. It seemed like my prayers of *Please, God, don't let him talk about Daniel* would go unanswered.

He began shakily. "As many of you know, our son Daniel was diagnosed with a brain tumor last week."

I exchanged a glance with Rachel.

"My son is in the hospital and we are awaiting the operation that will remove the tumor from his brain." He paused as if he couldn't believe the words that had just left his mouth or the reality they conveyed. Pursing his lips, he reached for the cup of water that is always placed on the podium for him. "This week I've been reminded that fear is not something felt only by children afraid of the dark. Fear is not something you automatically outgrow when you are old enough to buy your first car or graduate from college. Fear grows up with you. It follows you into the hospital room when your first child is born, and presents itself in the form of this immense need to protect the tiny human being whose life is now in your hands. The fear manifests itself as the feeling of helplessness that comes because you realize you can't keep every bad thing in the world away. You can only do so much to protect them. And it's love that fuels this fear, isn't it?" Dad paused as affirmative sounds filled the sanctuary. "My son is ill in a way I cannot heal. My wife and I have had to place him, our only son, into the hands of doctors. And we will need to trust them with his life. And that made me wonder... how much more does God look at humanity—at people He has created out of His love—and feel pain over the lack of belief, the rejection of the gospel message, the illnesses that run so deep?"

Many heads nodded, and Dad picked up gusto. He talked about how his recent experiences had given him new insight into the urgency God must feel as He views those who do not believe, and how we all should feel that urgency, too. It was a great sermon, if only he'd leave out some of the Daniel references that really hammered home the point that he was the most important thing and maybe always would be.

Every time I sighed or squirmed in my seat, Rachel touched my hand or gave me a reassuring glance as if soothing a spooked horse. I pictured her with both hands up like *whoa, girl* and it made me smile, just a little. I looked around the room at one point, trying to find Tracy. I spotted her sitting with a few other members of the church worship team. Tracy has a beautiful voice, which she puts to use every Sunday morning. You can bet her miss perfect act is a whole lot more convincing than mine. Even now, she looked completely angelic, with her hands folded and her back straight. She was earnestly listening to Dad while I struggled to keep my face free of the "Enough, already!" that was threatening to surface.

Mom was at the hospital that morning with Daniel,

and Dad was up there preaching, which left…me. My family was all scattered. I vaguely remembered a saying I heard in English class at the beginning of last year, something about how friends are the family you choose for yourself, and it suddenly made sense in a tangible way. I squeezed Rachel's hand and said a quick prayer that I could find more friends to turn into family, just in case mine fell apart.

As a guilty afterthought I tried to pray for Daniel too, but I didn't know what to say. *God, please help his tumor to disappear. God, please don't let Daniel die.*

After the service was over there came a fresh onslaught of the awkwardness. I'd had enough. Rachel went home— she never stayed for Sunday school after the service, but I always helped Mom teach her class of kindergarteners. I figured I might as well go help out, since I had to stick around anyway.

I walked across the patio and caught snatches of conversation that featured "…so sad about Daniel…" and "…need me to bring Annie to the hospital?" and "Brain surgery! I can't imagine…"

When I got to Mom's classroom, I found Mrs. Curtis rifling through a box of my mom's teaching materials. Her three-year-old daughter Olivia was in the corner messing around with the perfectly placed figures on Mom's story board, and she stared at me as I entered.

"What's up, Annie?" Mrs. Curtis said.

"Oh, sorry," was all I could think to say as I backed out of the room.

Of course. Mom wasn't here, so Mrs. Curtis was taking over. And why would she need help from the likes of me? Clearly Olivia had a handle on the whole story board situation, although I didn't think it was appropriate for Abraham to be upside-down in a body of water while a herd of nearby sheep partied around the burning bush.

The other kids my age usually attend one of the adult classes, but I sure didn't feel like doing that today, even if that's where Tracy would be. I pressed my ear to the closed door of the crying baby room next to the nursery and was relieved to hear absolutely nothing. This room was the escape hatch for moms with little babies who had the audacity to cry during church, but nobody really used it at this time of the day. I opened the door to find the room indeed empty, and I scuttled inside. It was always the quietest in this room. Well, it was quiet when there were no babies crying in it. I always felt pretty safe there too, like that maybe if the rest of the building was involved in some kind of freak accident, I'd be safe where all the babies hung out.

I curled up in a squashy chair and looked at the clock. It was only 10:40. That meant an hour of Sunday school plus at least another half-hour before Dad would be ready to leave. There was always a good chunk of time after church where Dad had to chat it up with everyone and shut the place down.

I sighed. I used to feel like our church was just the right size. It wasn't so small that everyone knew everyone else's business, and it wasn't so big that you got lost in the crowd. Except today, I would've given anything to feel absorbed and anonymous. Instead I felt painfully out of place and totally exposed, like I had a giant spotlight on my face. And no matter the size of the church, everyone always seemed to know *my* business, which was this: I did not belong here. Not today.

Maybe you should walk home. It's not like anybody would miss you. The thin, timid voice of my inner self-pity had grown louder that week. I impatiently brushed a tear away and scooted my chair into the only patch of sunlight streaming into the room from the single small window. *Don't be that girl, Annie, it absolutely won't make you feel better.*

I'm not sure when I drifted off, but when I woke up I noticed the patch of sunlight had moved; I was no longer in it. My attempt to unfold my legs and dislodge myself from the chair proved unsuccessful. I ended up on the floor, unable to get up due to fallen-asleep legs, when Travis walked in. Yes, really.

"Your dad is looking for you," Travis said, apparently familiar enough with my natural gracefulness to not appear overly surprised that I was sprawled out on the floor. I've been taking ballet since I was six years old, but somehow those skills don't overlap a whole lot with everyday life.

I looked at Travis with all the dignity I could muster, given the circumstances. "Are you sure? I didn't think he remembered I was here today, since my name isn't Daniel."

Travis arched one eyebrow and walked over to me, holding out a hand to help me up. He didn't ask me why I had been in the crying baby room by myself. I think he understood I was hiding. He didn't ask, didn't comment, and I knew he wouldn't repeat what I said. For once, I was overwhelmingly grateful for Travis's silence.

Chapter 7

On Monday Daniel was prepped for his surgery, which was happening first thing the next morning. He was as goofy as ever, trying to make a catapult out of two plastic spoons, three bendy straws, and a rubber band. It's like it was all just a big adventure to him. I was timid, and truth be told, felt every bit as awkward around him as our church members seemed to me. *Careful.* That's what we were. They were careful around me and I was careful around him. I wondered if Daniel felt as bothered by people tip-toeing around him as I did.

It was overly bright in the hospital wing where Daniel was, with too-sappy, poor likenesses of cartoon characters emblazoned on the walls. Noses were too big and eyes were too small, signature clothing was ever-so-slightly the wrong shade. Was everyone supposed to be confused and think they'd ended up at Disneyland instead of the hospital? Was that the idea? I already hated it there.

When Mom, Dad, and Tracy went to the cafeteria to get dinner for everyone, Daniel convinced one of the nurses to wheel the portable Nintendo into his room so we could play Mario Kart.

I glanced sideways at him mid-race. He was beating me by half a lap anyway. As usual he got to be Princess Peach, but this time I wasn't upset about it. I cleared my throat. "Aren't you scared about tomorrow?"

Princess Peach shot a red turtle shell out from behind her racecar, and it nailed me. "Not really. I'll be knocked out, and it's not like I can control anything that happens."

For someone his age, that was a sensible perspective. Never mind the fact that if I were in his place, I would be literally peeing my pants.

"Besides," he whispered, looking over his shoulder, "have you seen any of the other kids in this place? I have, and some of them are in pretty bad shape. I'm not sick the way they are. Like, there are some *really* sick people here."

Now, that was an interesting thing to say. Before I could ask him how in the world he didn't view his brain tumor as all that serious of a thing, he shot me a *told you so* look as a crying little girl in a wheelchair with an IV pole attached was pushed slowly down the hallway. I decided to let him go ahead and think what he wanted.

Daniel and I in our natural habitat usually fight over the remote or he endlessly tattles about me sneaking spoons of cookie dough to devour in my closet. Under most other circumstances I found him irritating as can be, but this was something different. I was allowed to be nice to him—soft and sisterly—under these terms and not have it be front page news. Daniel wasn't scared that night, and I admired him for it.

—————

The waiting that took place during Daniel's thirteen-hour surgery didn't feel like as big a deal to me as it was probably supposed to. My parents decided Tracy and I should try to preserve some normalcy, and they sent us to school that day while they waited at the hospital. I wondered about Daniel all day anyway. But whenever I thought too much about what was actually happening to him, my heart raced with panic and I had to force myself to think about something else. It was too terrible and creepy to think there were surgeons cutting into his actual *brain* for crying out loud. How had this all happened so fast?

To my parents it must have felt like a lifetime passed that day. After school I walked home, riding to the hospital with Tracy so we could wait out the remainder of the surgery as a family. Had it really only been a week since we all found out about this tumor? I sighed. *No Tuesday night babysitting for me tonight, I guess.*

When Tracy and I arrived at the hospital, Nora the second-shift receptionist barely glanced up from her trashy romance novel. "Hi, girls." She winked at me as I glanced sideways at her book. "Your parents are waiting in room 419." She waved off to her left and kept reading.

We made our way to the small room off the main waiting area and found our parents looking rigid and worried, pale with uncertainty and forced patience. My experience with all of this involved very little of the burden they carried, that much was obvious. While they could now rattle off a dizzying list of medical terms at the drop of a hat, all I knew was exactly what Dr. Gill had told all of us. Daniel had a cyst and tumor in his brain, and it might be a tricky task to get those out.

And although to me this was a straightforward matter of getting the tumor out so Daniel could heal and we'd all be back on our way to being a normal family, it was clear my parents saw things as not that simple. Daniel stood the chance of losing a great deal. Would he actually be able to go back to normal? What could he lose? My parents were like open books, mentally running through every plan B, every "What if?".

Every ten minutes or so, Mom would look at the clock and blink back tears. She sighed a lot but didn't speak to anyone. Dad looked numb, robotically putting his arm around Mom when he sensed she needed it.

"Let's say a prayer for Daniel," Dad said into the dense quiet about half an hour after Tracy and I arrived. We pulled our chairs into a circle, grabbed hands, and bowed our heads. I waited for Dad to say something, or Mom, but the only sounds were sniffles. I guess it was supposed to be the quiet kind of prayer, so I did my best. It was too scary to think about what the surgeons were actually doing, or picture what the operating room looked like. Too sad to think about how somewhere in this hospital Daniel was lying on a table, unconscious and vulnerable. Instead, I pictured a blanket of warm, twinkling light covering the hospital in a buttery glow of protection.

"Amen," said Dad after a few more minutes had gone by. We scooted our chairs back, and I realized Dad had to do this kind of thing a lot. Sit with the families, I mean. No doubt it was a whole lot scarier when it was your own family. But who stepped in when the pastor needed a shoulder?

There wasn't much to look at in the cramped, plain room. Around the surgery's twelve-hour mark, three hours after Tracy and I had arrived to sit vigil, I fell asleep right there in the chair. Tracy poked me in the ribs when Dr. Gill came in. I could see through the waiting room's small window that it had gotten dark outside.

My parents grew wild-eyed and I could see Mom squeeze Dad's hand so hard her knuckles turned white.

Dr. Gill smiled reassuringly. "Everything went well. I don't believe there's been any damage to Daniel's speech and language, but we'll need to run a few tests in a day or two to make sure. The anesthesia hasn't all worn off yet, but you can go and see him."

My parents sagged with relief. They looked like they hadn't slept in days.

"I'll call everyone and let them know," Dad said.

Mom looked at him, and he froze. She wanted to see Daniel *now*, but I think she was scared to go alone.

"I'll do it," Tracy said.

I knew she'd be calling both sets of grandparents first—my mom's parents who lived all the way across the country but had still offered to come stay with us; and my dad's parents, who lived an hour away and would probably drive out tomorrow to see Daniel. I knew my grandparents would dutifully share the update with our aunts and uncles scattered here and there, telling them everything had gone according to plan. Some lived close enough to visit, too. I knew after that, Tracy would call the person in charge of the prayer network at church this month, and the good news would spread. I could imagine a giant, collective sigh of relief.

Dad nodded his appreciation to Tracy as he and Mom crept out of the waiting room. I watched them go one way and Tracy another, no doubt she was heading somewhere with better cell reception. I decided to follow my parents down the too-bright, too-quiet corridor of the ICU, my shoes squeaking on the white tile. When I got to my brother's room I ran my fingers along the nameplate, gazing in disbelief at the *Daniel Spencer* written there before peeking in.

My parents had entered the dim room, looking smaller and more tired than they ever had before. Mom choked back quiet sobs as she reached out to touch Daniel's face.

Dad was fighting the tears, I could tell. Whether they were tears of relief or anger or disbelief, I didn't know.

And then there was Daniel. It was surreal to see my little brother, always so lively, lying there blank and silent. His eyes were closed, his thin arms hooked up to all sorts of machines going *beep-beep-beep* out of time with each other. Much of his head was wrapped in white gauze, and his whole face looked swollen beyond recognition. I couldn't stop staring.

I felt inappropriate and out of place there, spying on them this way. Watching Mom lightly stroke Daniel's bandaged head, I got a random flashback of her tending to Smokey when he was so weak and small. Mom and her tireless care. I think she wished there was some way she could pitch in and make Daniel stronger, but this was beyond her skills of administering heating pads and eye droppers filled with kitten medication. It was too big and maybe she felt helpless. Looking at Daniel from the doorway, maybe I felt helpless, too.

I don't know how long I stood in the doorway before Tracy tip-toed up and squeezed my shoulder. As usual there was kindness in her probing eyes, but I didn't let her stare too intently because she was always finding things out that way that I didn't want her to know. "Your face is completely white. Let's just go in."

All at once the reality of the situation sunk in. This was really happening, there was nowhere to hide, and there was no denying it now. She took my hand and in we went, settling by the foot of Daniel's hospital bed.

"It's a miracle, really," Mom said, her voice steadied by force and pitched a little higher. "At any other hospital they wouldn't have had the skilled staff to operate on this type of tumor. And his speech and language will most likely be just fine. A miracle. Really."

We all nodded, though I wasn't sure if she was talking to us or trying to drown out her own worry with manufactured gratitude, commanding the best outcome for Daniel through sheer force of will.

I was quiet. I felt so awkward standing by his hospital bed not knowing what to do or say. The doctor had said he was okay, but he didn't look like it to me. This was so intense, and I didn't trust myself to say anything without crying. I had to look away from Daniel's swollen little face...I caught sight instead of something black clutched in Daniel's right hand. It was furry and I saw a pink plastic nose and part of a whisker poking out from between his fingers. It was the black Beanie Baby panther I had bought him from the hospital's gift shop the day before. Mom followed my gaze and noticed the panther, too. She reached over to tug gently at it, but it didn't budge. I wondered if he'd clung to that thing the whole surgery. I wondered why he was clinging to it now. Maybe it was the "I love you" he deserved from me and didn't get nearly often enough.

Chapter 8

Getting up the next morning to go to school proved to be difficult. How could I go on like life was normal, and pretend my brother wasn't lying in a hospital bed across town? Mom and Dad had both stayed overnight at the hospital, and the house felt empty without them.

Early this morning Mom had sent a text to Tracy and me. *Daniel's awake!* An accompanying picture showed a small, bandaged, swollen Daniel with his eyes barely open.

I trudged to school with the image of Daniel's face burned into my mind, and was only a little relieved to see Rachel bounding up to me as I walked into the main building for homeroom. "You didn't text me yesterday. How did the surgery go?"

Our homerooms are across the hall from each other, and when both of us are on time we usually walk together.

"Things went fine," I practically shouted to be heard over the noise of the hall. "He's awake now and going to be fine, but it was scary. He looks so…" I shook my head. I couldn't explain the intricacies of my family's trauma in this noisy hallway. Rachel cocked her head and started to say something, but was immediately drowned out by the bell instead. "Later," I said as she gave me a light shove toward my homeroom and turned to scurry toward her own.

I walked into the classroom and looked around at all the other kids who were laughing and talking and sure didn't look like they had a brother in the hospital, like I did. Or maybe they had even worse stuff going on—I guess you never know. But one thing was for sure, I felt different. I wondered if anybody else could tell.

Rachel and I didn't get to talk in second period math, either. We were handed a pop quiz the moment we walked in the door, and I felt the heart-pounding dread of yet another life event I was unprepared for.

I sunk into my chair and let my backpack fall to the ground in a heap, but as my eyes scanned the page I noticed something. I could do this stuff. It was no different than the homework I'd had lots more time to do since the house was quiet. I took out a pencil and got to work.

When I caught up with Rachel at lunchtime, I was feeling pretty good. It was a relief to have a small oasis of good news. I'd gotten last week's English quiz back last period and was shocked to see the "A-" displayed above the "Great work!"

"Wow, look at you!" said Rachel when I showed her my paper. "Closet genius. Who knew?"

I grinned at her. "School just seems easier."

"Well, it's probably a lot easier to deal with school than everything else that's going on right now."

I shrugged. "I guess."

Rachel beamed at me. "I'll bet you aced that quiz in math today, too. You were done even before I was."

The weather was sunny and cheerful, and I still had fourth period dance class to look forward to. We had a recital coming up the following week, and we'd all been working hard to prepare.

As I opened my dance locker, I couldn't help smiling as I took out my toe shoes.

Ballet felt like the only place on earth left untouched by all things related to the tumor. It was the one aspect of my life where nobody expected me to act a certain way; I could be happy or silly or sad or quiet, and nobody faulted me for it. It was a place where I was free and I didn't need to hide.

I was also pretty excited about this recital, because I'd been working hard since the end of last school year and all summer on a solo, and was hoping to finally get to perform it. I stretched out after the day's warm-up. We were running through everyone's solos today to see which dances would be in the recital, and my solo was last. Instead of feeling nervous, I was excited to perform it.

The hour passed quickly, and soon it was time for me

to take center stage. As the music began and I started to dance, I could feel the tension of the past week subsiding. My favorite part of the routine was coming up, the fouetté en tournant I'd worked so hard to perfect. I took a deep breath. Up on one pointed toe with the other leg parallel to the stage and my ankle crossing at the knee, I spread my arms in the delicate arc Madame taught me, and I kicked my leg to propel through the quick circle. As I spun around, I snapped my head back to the clock on the far wall that I'd chosen as my spot to watch so it was easier to keep my balance. Again and again, six times total I spun, and never got dizzy. I felt light and free.

My body moved easily through the choreography, the grand jetés connecting to each other like dancing in water. Only when the dance was finished, only when my body was stretched in the open arc of my final pose, did I break my gaze and look out into the darkness where the audience would be next Wednesday night.

I slowly dropped my arms to my sides, waiting for my eyes to adjust as I tried to look past the blinding spotlight into the seats. I could see the single silhouette of Madame Kaessler, my dance instructor.

She stood tall, her body still, and I could just barely see her head nodding slowly. "Excellent," she said in her elegant French accent that flowed and lilted. "You have worked hard, and you are ready."

I smiled to myself as I went backstage to pack my stuff up. The attention filled me with a burst of accomplishment.

It felt wonderful that someone had seen me for me, and not as Daniel's sister. Immediately this thought collided with the memory of his face all drugged up and exhausted, and I felt like a disloyal brat. Was it okay to be happy now that the worst was over and Daniel was going to be fine? If not now, when?

When I got home after school, Mrs. Diaz was there to drive me to the hospital. Tracy had an away track meet that afternoon and she couldn't miss it. She'd worked it out with her coach to drive herself and leave right after her events, instead of waiting around and coming home with the team on the bus. Did Tracy keep seeing the image of post-surgery Daniel in her mind, and did she feel bad for trying to retain some pieces of her normal life? I made a mental note to ask her later.

"Good day at school?" Mrs. Diaz asked.

I nodded. I was instantly transformed into dutifully serious, somber Annie. In the old days I would've said it was a great day. But I felt like telling her about it would make me sound like the selfish sister who was happy even though her brother was going through something terrible. I thought about telling Mrs. Diaz how lately I was feeling a little overlooked, but then I thought that would give off the impression I didn't care enough about what was going on with my own family. So we ended up making small talk the entire way about her family's new puppy.

When we rolled up to the hospital, she reached for something in the back. "I can't believe I almost forgot!" She plunked a plastic container full of coins into my hands. "A little vending machine survival stash."

"Score!" I exclaimed, a real laugh breaking loose. "I'm so not sharing this."

Mrs. Diaz's warm smile radiated out at me as I waved and closed the door.

Inside the hospital I was starting to know my way around. I strode past the nurses' station in the ICU, exchanging glances and polite, stiff smiles with a few I recognized as I walked by.

I crept into Daniel's room to find Mom asleep in the chair and Daniel propped up in bed, groggy and staring warily at some orange Jell-O on the tray in front of him. Already he looked a little less pale and swollen than he had right after his surgery. His eyes settled on me and he raised his eyebrows in recognition.

I approached his hospital bed with caution, side-stepping the formidable sea of tubes, wires, and cords. Was it safe to try and hug him, or would I accidentally unplug something and hurt him? I settled on a small wave and a big, fake smile meant to disguise my shock at how different he still looked. "Good news! The doctors did actually find that you have a brain in there. So I guess I lost a bet."

Daniel did something approaching an eye-roll and groaned. "First time I've heard that one. Not."

I smiled. "How are you feeling?"

With effort, Daniel lifted his arm from his side and gave me a weak thumbs-up.

"Well, you look good. Kind of like...a human Q-tip."

He slowly patted his bulbous, bandaged head. "That's better than you look." He then showed me how he was mastering the ancient art of the hospital bed controls all by himself. Just Daniel being Daniel.

Soon he got tired and dozed off, and I settled into the chair by the window. I looked around at our new home away from home and noticed several cards propped up on a table. Two small bunches of balloons were standing guard in corners of the room, and I zoned out watching one mylar balloon, caught in the air conditioning draft, spin lazily. On one side: *This balloon will help you get well!* ...and on the other side came the punchline: *It's full of heal-ium!*

Dad came into the room with some hospital gunk posing as food for Mom. He gently nudged her awake. "Come on, you've gotta eat something."

As Mom stretched and made a face at the mashed chicken nuggets and fries, Dad sat down at the edge of Daniel's bed. They didn't notice I was in the room until I shifted in my chair and said, "So, you've had some visitors?"

Mom smiled a tired smile, and Dad said "Yes, it's been a pretty steady stream all day. Uncle Paul and Aunt Barb came with Grandma and Grandpa this morning, and a few people from church after that."

I nodded. "That's good. How long do they think it'll take for Daniel to recover enough to go home?"

Mom shrugged and stifled a yawn. "For now they have to wait for the swelling to go down and run some tests to make sure they got the whole tumor. Maybe a week, if all goes well."

"Wow. A whole other week?" Feeling brave, I took a deep breath. "My dance recital's next week. Wednesday, remember? And Madame said I could perform my solo." The room was quiet, and my voice didn't fill it. "Think you guys can make it?"

Dad looked at me, studying my face.

"We'll see," said Mom, her eyes glued to sleeping Daniel.

Chapter 9

Life settled into a new routine. Each day at the hospital Daniel got a little stronger, less swollen, with more of that Daniel spark in his eyes. Still, there had been no talk of him coming home. People from church had organized a meal rotation for our family, and Tracy and I had become experts on who made the best casseroles. I floated around between school, home, and the hospital. A couple of afternoons after school I even got to escape the hospital and hang out at Rachel's house instead. It was a welcome change, although Rachel and her parents sometimes studied me like I was a museum spectacle: *Still Life of Suspended Family Trauma*.

Before I knew it, it was the night of the recital. It felt like the whole week had flown by at warp speed and deposited me breathless in a corner backstage, nervously flexing my toe shoes in my hands as I waited for the recital to begin. From where I sat, I could see most of the faces in the growing audience. No familiar faces yet. No Mom and Dad. I hadn't mentioned my recital again, for fear they would think I was being insensitive. But they always came to my recitals. At least, they used to. Deep down I had expected at least one of them to show up.

A sudden giggle burst through my consciousness, and I was aware of Rachel crouching down next to me.

"Yo." She waved a hand in front of my face and laughed. "I don't think I've ever seen you this nervous in the entire time I've known you. What's up?"

"I'm not nervous at all," I lied. The pit in my stomach grew and I avoided Rachel's eyes.

Onstage, Madame Kaessler began the program. Rachel squeezed my right ballet shoe. "Lace these things up, kid, you'll do great. You always do."

The evening flew by in a blur, and then I was being ushered through the curtains as my name was called. Stunned, I made my way to center stage under dark blue lights. My heart pounded as I waited for the music to begin. *Stage fright?* This wasn't me. Tonight I wanted my movements to carry me away, beyond the probing eyes of so many faces out there, so many unfamiliar faces.

The dancing was automatic, I felt no freedom and there was no magic. The lyrics of Mariah Carey's "Hero" swirled around me as if I was hearing them for the first time.

I didn't realize there were tears on my face until my solo was over. I came to my senses as the last echoes of the song floated away, and was shocked to notice the ending pose felt far too vulnerable to me. I wanted to hide—to curl up in a ball. Not stand there wearing my pain etched on my face for the world to see.

The audience applauded as I shifted to a low bow, trying my best to smile as I hurried offstage. Feeling the overwhelming need to be invisible, I changed back into my street clothes while the other dancers buzzed excitedly all around me.

"Annie, you did great!" one of them said. I smiled and murmured a return.

Out in front of the auditorium is where my parents usually met me after a performance. Tonight, there was only Rachel and her mom.

"That was excellent, Annie," Rachel's mom said. "I can tell you spent lots of time working on your dance."

"Thanks—I'm glad you guys came." I said it as warmly as I could, although I felt distracted. "Have you seen my parents around anywhere?"

They looked at each other and Rachel pointed to her left, where I could make out my mom's shadowy figure sitting in the family car parked a short distance off.

I blinked back tears as I waved goodbye to Rachel and her mom, then jogged to the car. My parents hadn't come to see me, after all. Mom was just there to pick me up. I dropped into the front seat and looked into her face, expecting an explanation. Her features were frozen solid and she was staring straight ahead.

My heart sank. *Well, they don't care to see you dance,*

but at least you don't have to walk home, rasped a cruel voice inside. I couldn't stop the tears from falling now, and I turned to speak.

Mom cut me short with words of her own. "Dr. Gill ran some scans on your brother today." Her shaky voice tapered into an overly controlled whisper. "They didn't get the whole tumor out, so they want to operate on Daniel again as soon as he's recovered a little more."

I looked out the car window and held my breath. *Another* surgery? Oh wow. My brain tried to pick this information apart, but I couldn't think past the mountain of hurt feelings crowding into my heart because my family didn't want to see me dance.

Mom had her car keys clutched in her lap, but when she tried to start the car they fell out of her shaking hands. That did it. Mom howled in frustration, which scared me so much I felt the shiver of adrenaline travel the entire length of my body. I'd never seen her like this before.

Mom began to sob. "Looking at your brother, and knowing how much pain he's in, I can't imagine having to tell him he's got to go through it all again." She buried her face in her hands.

Daniel wasn't the only one who was going to have to go through it all again. I whispered "Sorry, Mom," and listened to her cry.

We drove home without speaking, and randomly I thought about our little tradition after every dance recital to go out for ice cream. And sometimes Tracy and Daniel would come too, but there would be no ice cream this time.

When we pulled into the driveway I slipped out of the car and into the house, where I went straight to my room and closed the door. The doorway to Tracy's bedroom stood dark and empty, so there would be nobody to commiserate with. Had I even told Tracy about my recital? I couldn't remember. Tossing my dance bag onto the floor, I turned off the light and crawled into bed fully clothed, pulling the covers up to my eyes.

I hadn't heard Mom come in the house. She'd probably gone right back to the hospital. Was I completely alone?

The wind swirled the moonlight in the tree branches outside my window, casting mournful, twisted shadows on my bed. I had myself a good cry. I couldn't believe we all had to go through the uncertainty and stress of another surgery, just when things were getting better. But didn't I deserve one night in the spotlight anyway? One minute where they would look at me and see *me*? Was I about to disappear completely?

You're special, Annie. We're proud of you, Annie.

Why couldn't they just say it?

Chapter 10

The next morning before school, I poured out my whole sob story on Rachel. I dumped out all the hurt feelings over being invisible in my family, and told her Daniel had to have a whole other surgery.

She listened with wide eyes and both hands covering her mouth. Then she pounced on me with a ferocious hug. "Of all the times to run out of Peeps," she muttered. "I'm so sorry. Poor Daniel!"

At the hospital that afternoon I shoved myself as far into the corner of Daniel's room as possible. I sat there immersed in math homework, staring out the window, or buried in my favorite comfort book, *The Giver* by Lois Lowry. Anything to forget where I actually was, and stop all the worries that were coming right back at us. I smiled dutifully when Uncle Paul came to visit after donating blood for Daniel's second surgery, my parents taking turns hugging him and clasping his hands in the silent *thank you* Daniel wouldn't have understood.

My parents had decided not to tell Daniel about the second surgery he had to have. It didn't feel great, but it was probably for the best. Even *his* optimism had its limitations, and all you had to do was look at the kid to know he was in pain. His head was still swollen, and sometimes when he opened his eyes they looked vacant from exhaustion and too much pain medication. Maybe that's just something that happens when you pour so much suffering into a ten-year-old. But he could also sit up on his own, eat on his own, and had to be stopped multiple times a day from peeling back the gauze to show off his battle scars from the surgery.

I kept my distance, watching from my corner of the hospital room and not trusting my face to hide the bad news that he was going under the knife again. It was terrible knowing things were going to get worse before they got better, when Daniel didn't.

Daniel's second surgery took place Friday afternoon while I was in school. I was sitting in third period English when I got a note that one of the school counselors wanted to see me, and I obediently trudged up to her office.

I handed my slip to the office assistant and took a seat in the empty waiting room. It was quiet except for the sound of her typing, and pretty soon the door to my right swung open and a graying head popped out. It was an interestingly shaped head, the kind where the forehead is too big and the whole face tapers down into this teeny chin.

She peered over rhinestone-encrusted glasses at me. "Are you Annie?" It occurred to me I had never seen this person before in my entire time at this school. She wasn't one of the regular academic counselors. Perhaps she was the counselor in charge of only the big stuff, and they kept her squirreled away in case of emergencies.

I nodded, stood up, and made my way into her office. She closed the door and motioned for me to sit in the chair opposite her desk. She was a tiny woman, shorter than I was. She wore a black suit begging on her behalf that she be taken seriously. She sat, folded her arms on top of her desk, and leaned all the way forward. "Annie, I got a call from your mother a few minutes ago. She wanted us to let you know that your brother will be having his surgery today while you're in school."

I nodded at her numbly. This wasn't exactly news. I think the counselor expected she was dropping some kind of a bomb on me, because I saw her nudge a box of Kleenex to the edge of her desk. After a minute or so of silence and me not taking the Kleenex bait, she spoke up. "Do you want to talk about it?"

"Not really." I didn't want to be rude, but what good could come of talking to her about it? She didn't know who I was, and she didn't know anything about my family. I also suspected she didn't know a great deal about brain tumors.

She nodded slowly, then stood up. "Well, I'll be outside if you need me. Take as much time as you need."

I watched her creep out of the office and close the door gently behind her, like Rachel and I did when there was a baby sleeping in the nursery. But I was no baby, so what exactly was I supposed to do in here? How long would I have to sit before the counselor was convinced I was not a troubled, heartless child? Wouldn't it be funny if I sat in there for the rest of the day? I'm sure she'd have to get into her office at some point, and maybe when she did I'd be sitting at her desk and I'd demand she leave my office at once. She'd be so shocked that probably her bedazzled glasses would fall off her face. The mental image made me laugh and I'm positive they heard me through the closed door.

Maybe they'd think I was crying instead, and be satisfied I was normal. But actually, did I care what they thought about me? Also, people should be careful about saying things they don't mean…things like "Take as much time as you need," and "Everything's going to be okay." Nobody can actually know how much time you need, and nobody can promise things will be fine when they really don't know.

After a few minutes, I got bored and gave up my claim on the counselor's office. It would be lunchtime soon anyway.

The counselor and the office assistant were whispering to each other, and stopped when they saw me.

"Thanks, ladies," I said, giving them a small salute and excusing myself from the room. It was fun not caring what people thought.

Tracy and I hung out at home after school that day, waiting for news about the surgery. She had been despondent and showed up for only a quick hospital visit once Mom told her Daniel was in for another procedure he didn't know about. It turns out the two of us are pretty lousy actresses, so there goes *that* career path. I told her how the school counselor had acted like telling me about Daniel's second surgery was some kind of deep and shocking revelation.

She barked a laugh and shook her head. "I got called out from class, too. I think Mom must've called our schools and told them what was going on, as an excuse in case we freaked out in class or something."

I rolled my eyes up to the ceiling. "So what you're telling me is I missed a golden opportunity to freak out with no consequences? Although, I'm pretty sure the entire school office now thinks I have emotional problems."

"You probably do."

I shot Tracy a fake glare, and she laughed. Of course, I could never *really* be mad at her. I wasn't even that upset she hadn't come to my dance recital. It turned out she was stuck at work covering a shift for someone who had been helping cover for her a lot lately. Besides, she had brought home half of a leftover cheesecake, so all was forgiven.

Dad finally called and said everything went well, and that Daniel was resting. There were some tests the doctors would need to run when he woke up, but for now everything seemed great. The surgery hadn't taken as long as the first one had, and I registered how it didn't feel like as big a deal as the first one, either. Was it weird that brain surgery was becoming so common in the Spencer household that I barely batted an eye? Maybe I was just impatient to put this whole thing behind us so we could finally get back to normal. Tracy and I celebrated the good news by polishing off the rest of a chicken and rice casserole. Thank you, church ladies!

Chapter 11

The next morning, Tracy and I hopped in her car to go to the hospital.

"I wonder what his recovery will be like this time around," she said. "He bounced back pretty fast the first time. Maybe in a week or two everybody will be able to come home."

We smiled at each other. It felt like forever since we had all been home. Would it go right back to being like it was before, though? Was this something that would be hanging over our family from now on, and could the tumor come back?

I pushed my worries to the side as Tracy and I strode toward the ICU waiting room. As we approached, a nurse came out to meet us. "I'm sorry, girls. Dr. Gill wanted to talk with just your parents this time." She motioned to an empty corner of the waiting room, outside of Dr. Gill's closed door.

Tracy and I glanced at each other as we slowly sat

down. Something felt off. How long would we have to sit there and wonder how bad the news was?

Not long. Dr. Gill's office door creaked open and out came my parents. Mom was crying softly and Dad looked stunned. Tracy and I stood up, and when they saw us, Dad reached out his arms and took us both into a tight squeeze.

"What's going on?" Tracy rasped. But I couldn't take my eyes off my mom's face. By the time we all found a private corner of the waiting room to talk, my mind was racing through every possible scenario that would warrant this type of reaction from them. My stomach clenched. I couldn't remember the last thing I'd said to Daniel. Suddenly that was very important to me. He knew I loved him, right?

Dad took a deep breath. "So, it's not great news."

Well, obviously! I wanted to shout.

"They took some scans after the surgery, and ran some tests to confirm. While they do believe they got the whole tumor out this time, it's clear Daniel had a stroke during the surgery."

Stroke?

Yes, I had heard correctly. I tried hard to focus as Dad explained that one of the many tiny blood vessels surrounding Daniel's tumor had gotten nicked while the remainder of the tumor was being removed.

"What does that mean?" asked Tracy. "He's going to be okay, right?"

Mom's voice came out small. "The doctors won't know

the full extent of the damage for a few more days. Just now Dr. Gill told us Daniel has some paralysis on his entire left side."

She choked a little on the word "paralysis." So did I. Tracy gasped.

Dad spoke. "He said it's a type of paralysis. A one-sided weakness called hemiparesis. The doctors aren't sure how much Daniel will recover, and it's a long road. He'll have to work hard, and even then, he may not make a full recovery."

We sat in wounded silence, taking it in. *Daniel is alive* came the one ray of good news my brain clung to.

We all filed out of the waiting room, and my parents led us to Daniel's room. My breath caught when I saw him— he looked worse than he had after the first surgery. His face was so swollen that his eyes had all but disappeared. His head was wrapped with even more gauze. He was so still it was hard to imagine he was ever able to jump and play and laugh. Was this really my brother in this hospital bed?

Dad picked up his worn leather Bible from Daniel's bedside table, opened it, and began to read Psalm 23. "'The Lord is my shepherd, I shall not be in want. He makes me lie down in green pastures, He leads me beside quiet waters, He restores my soul. He guides me in paths of righteousness for His name's sake. Even though I walk through the valley of the shadow of death, I will fear no evil, for You are with me; Your rod and Your staff, they comfort me. You prepare a table before me in the presence of my enemies. You anoint my head with oil; my cup overflows. Surely goodness and love will follow me all the days of my life, and I will dwell in the house of the Lord forever.'"

I watched as Dad brushed away tears and Tracy and Mom held each other, crying quietly. It was all too much to bear, and I found my feet backing slowly out of the room. Too much sadness, too many days and nights spent watching my parents cry over their little boy in his hospital bed.

Inside, my thoughts were screaming. *It's never going to be the same again! It isn't fair!* Hot tears sprang to my eyes and raced down my cheeks. How stupid I'd been to come here looking for good news, thinking we'd all be a normal family soon.

I had no idea where my feet were carrying me. Just away. As I careened through the ICU corridor I didn't see Dr. Gill until it was almost too late. He strode quickly down the hall toward me but no way did I feel like running into him, *Dr. Brain-nicker*. Panicked, I ducked into the nearest room and closed the door behind me before I could be spotted.

As I turned and took in the sun-streaked room—its setup a backward layout from Daniel's—my eyes skimmed over the many hook-ups and medical gadgets before I finally noticed the room's inhabitants.

There were two beds crammed into this room instead

of just the one that was in Daniel's. And in each of these beds was a girl, neither looking much older than I was. The girl in the bed closest to the door was bald, her face blazing scarlet and her dark eyes set in an unapologetic scowl. Her face and body were a complicated roadmap of tubes so I was unsure where to look so I wouldn't seem rude.

As I struggled to come up with an excuse for barging into their room, she roared her greeting. "What do *you* want?"

"Don't be like that," the other girl said. "You always scare away my visitors."

I quickly took in the second girl. She had bright green eyes and lovely red hair, with curls that spiraled delightfully out of control.

She looked at me. "Don't mind her, she's always crabby until she gets her meds." She laughed as the first girl stuck her tongue out and snatched up a book from her bedside table. "My name's Jenna, she's Amanda. What's your name?"

I noticed as I came closer to Jenna's bed that both her legs and one of her arms were suspended in casts. "I'm Annie."

"Hi, Annie. I know, I look bizarre." Jenna rolled her eyes toward her plaster-covered arm. "Like half human, half paper doll."

Was it okay to laugh at that? Too late.

"I was in a boating accident," Jenna explained. "I'm all

screwed up inside. What's your story?" There was laughter and expectation in her eyes as she stared back at me.

I felt like I could tell this stranger anything. And where else could I go, anyway? "I'm…hiding from a doctor," I began.

Jenna laughed. "Ha! Well, I'm sorry to tell you you're in the wrong place. Every time I turn around I've got doctors poking and prodding me without so much as a 'Whoops, did that hurt?' or a 'Sure, I'll give you my phone number.'"

I felt my face break into a real smile. Not an I'm-okay-so-don't-ask-me-if-I-want-to-talk-about-anything smile.

Jenna's eyes glittered. "So are you an escapee, or what? Are we harboring a runaway from the psych ward?"

Amanda sighed from behind her book. "Like they even have one of those at this hospital."

My smile faded. "Not *my* doctor, my brother's."

"Oh." She was clearly disappointed that the truth was less dramatic. "Well, what's your brother in for?"

I answered solemnly, automatically. "Brain tumor."

Jenna's eyes widened a little, and out of the corner of my eye I saw movement as Amanda lowered her book. "Is he okay?" Jenna asked.

I shifted my weight from one foot to the other. Now both girls were staring at me, unblinking. Jenna's eyes were wide with concern, but Amanda stared through me, like she was daring me to come up with a sob story worse than hers.

"It was operable," I began, my vocal cords shifting to the Daniel-talk setting where all of the answers to these questions lived. "He had a golf-ball-sized tumor and a cyst in the middle of his brain, and actually he had to have two operations because they didn't get the whole tumor out the first time." I took a deep breath, feeling like I was a separate girl in the room watching this jabbering idiot go on and on about her brother. "And we just found out he had a stroke during his second surgery, and he's sort of paralyzed, I guess? So I don't know if he's okay. Nobody knows much of anything yet. But he looks awful."

Jenna sighed. "Whoa. I'm so sorry."

In one sharp movement, Amanda covered her face back up with her book and resumed her "I don't care about anything" routine. Pretty convincing, except I could tell her book was now upside-down. Jenna noticed it too, raising her eyebrows sky-high at me as I pursed my lips to keep from laughing.

Jenna's face neutralized back into gentle concern. "It's going to be okay, you know. It's scary, especially at first. My family is super freaked out about me being here, too. But it's all going to be okay."

I smiled and whispered "Thanks." I can't explain why I believed her, or why the caring attention of this stranger seeped in below my sadness in a way nobody else had achieved.

"So, tell me all about you." Jenna continued, upbeat

and sparkling. "There's never anything good on this TV and I'm so bored."

I laughed and sat down on the chair next to her bed. The angry thoughts that had sizzled in my brain just minutes ago had vanished. "Oh I'm SO interesting." I gave her the "all about me" first day of school bullet points: pastor's kid, middle kid, dancer, reader, lover of interesting pens.

When I was done, I gave her *ta-da* jazz hands and she applauded. "You know what? You *are* interesting. Feel free to come hide here anytime."

I laughed, warmth flooding my heart. "How about you? Are you interesting?"

It turned out Jenna was exactly six months older than I was and lived in Tempe, the next city over. I also found out she had a twin brother named Owen.

"A twin?!" I exclaimed, imagining myself skipping down the lane holding hands with a double. "What's that like?"

"Uh, less cutesy than you think, I'm sure. Most people don't know we're twins. But it's just me and Owen, no other brothers or sisters, so he might as well just be a regular brother."

I nodded, glancing back toward Amanda, who had given up on her book and was pretending to be asleep. The scowl still hadn't left her face.

The door banged open and in came a nurse I

recognized, dragging a cart bearing lunch trays from the hospital cafeteria.

It was Nurse Joy, the one who'd arranged for my mom to get a cot in Daniel's room so she'd be more comfortable. "You have a visitor, I see." She smiled at me as she expertly propped up a magically awake Amanda and began to situate her tray in front of her.

Jenna beamed at me. "This is my new friend Annie. She's on loan from the lobotomy section of this place."

Amanda shook her bald head in frustration, rolling her eyes for good measure.

Nurse Joy laughed and made her way over to Jenna's bed with a tray. "I know who she is. Annie, I'm so sorry about your brother. He's such a sweet kid and we're all pulling for him to make a full recovery." Nurse Joy's eyes were kind. They were always kind, which was probably why she was one of Daniel's favorites. She reached out to squeeze my shoulder.

Jenna interrupted, banging her fork onto the hard plastic tray. "Hey lady, don't forget you've got sick people to take care of here."

Nurse Joy tapped her foot and stared at the ceiling, hands on hips. "How was it that Jenna likes her tea? I don't remember. Maybe I'll dump some raspberry flavoring in there, because that's what normal people like."

Jenna made a gagging sound and draped her good arm over her eyes. "No! Anything but raspberry. I promise I'll be good."

"Works every time." Nurse Joy grinned as she placed a tall glass of iced tea onto Jenna's tray. "Please don't judge me for this." She winked at me, pulling several sugar packets from her uniform pocket and placing them next to the tea. "This is the only thing that keeps this girl so sweet. Otherwise my life would be miserable."

Jenna looked up, indignant. "What's so weird about wanting sweet tea that's actually just sweet instead of flavored with some gross, artificial stuff that doesn't taste like the kind of fruit it's posing as?"

Nurse Joy dragged the empty cart back out, shaking her head and closing the door behind her.

Amanda chimed in through a mouthful of mashed potatoes. "Maybe it's the fact that you also dump like fifty-seven packets of sugar into plain water, and that's just sick."

Jenna gasped. "Now you work for the CIA? And you didn't tell me?"

"Oh definitely," Amanda said, rolling her eyes. "I'm compiling a special report about humans who think they're hummingbirds. Fascinating stuff."

Jenna's eyes danced. "You know what? I think Bob would love to see you again. In fact, I'm sure of it."

Amanda dropped her fork onto her plate with a clang, and raised a hand to cover her eyes. "Don't you dare think about showing me that while I'm eating."

"I named my gut-slice Bob," Jenna told me. "I got it from the propeller of the boat. Want to see?"

"I'll pass." I was laughing on the outside but cringing on the inside. She was basically Daniel in teenage girl form. What was it with people in this hospital wanting to show everyone their injuries? "And anyway, I should probably get back before someone misses me."

Jenna smiled and nodded. "Come see me again soon, yeah?"

"I will," I said, smiling at her and giving Amanda a little wave—which she ignored—as I left.

The hospital corridor felt different as I walked back to Daniel's room. I had a friend in this bright, faceless hospital. A friend who was part hummingbird and part paper doll, with a twin brother named Owen and a "gut-slice" named Bob.

I guess a weird friend is better than no friend.

The magic vanished as soon as I set foot back in Daniel's room, as if a heavy black blanket of despair cloaked the entire place. He looked even more swollen and listless than I remembered. Mom, Dad, and Tracy sat in chairs around his bed looking absolutely crushed. And scared. They looked so scared that it made Jenna's laughing smile feel like it lived on the moon instead of just down the hall.

Chapter 12

It took three whole days for the doctors to realize the full extent of what Daniel had lost. Just like after the first surgery, Daniel was pretty drugged up and had to be fed his meals. But this time around, the swelling in his face didn't go down at all on the left side.

"It's because of the stroke," Dr. Gill explained on Monday afternoon. He came in to check on Daniel and give the whole family a progress update, and Mom had asked about the swelling. "And since the stroke occurred on the right side of Daniel's brain, which controls the left side of his body, Daniel will have to re-learn how to walk. This is because he's lost some muscle tone in his left arm, left leg, and the left side of his face. He also has some blind spots in his left field of vision that may improve with time and physical therapy, or may be permanent."

Permanent?

Next to me, Tracy shifted in her seat. Her sudden movement caught me off guard and I felt my whole body jerk, accidentally knocking over the rolling table that held the remnants of Daniel's lunch. The whole thing went clattering to the floor, and as Mom and Tracy rushed to upend it, I caught sight of Daniel. His face had contorted in such a way that at first I couldn't figure out what was going on. His eyes, vacant and numb, were nearly lost in the persistent swelling that was his cheeks. One side of his mouth stretched out, curved upward, while the other side remained at rest. It was the first time Daniel—the new Daniel—smiled at me.

I didn't wait long before my next visit with Jenna. This time the door to her room was open and the first thing I noticed was Amanda's empty bed. I glanced at the name-plates on the door and saw Amanda's was still there. It was right below…Walker? Jenna *Walker*? Her last name was Walker and she couldn't walk. Wow. Rough.

The second thing I noticed was that Jenna already had visitors. A woman sat in the chair beside Jenna, fussing over a button on the side of the bed, and there was a red-haired boy standing by the window.

I stood in the doorway and watched as the woman repeatedly pressed the button, oblivious to the fact that the button actually controlled the placement of the slings elevating Jenna's legs.

"Mom! Mom! Mom!" said an annoyed Jenna in time with the button pushes, while the woman said "I don't understand why this isn't working. Isn't it supposed to be one of those adjust-o-matic beds? For what we're paying to keep you here—"

My eyes fell to the boy, and I knew at once he must be Jenna's twin brother Owen. As he noticed me in the doorway, I saw they shared those green eyes as well as the red corkscrew hair.

Jenna beckoned me in. "Annie, this is my crazy mom and my grumpy brother. Crazy, Grumpy, this is Annie."

Crazy took a break from the button and gave me a once-over, her own green eyes twinkling. "Hello, Annie, is your mother around? I'd like to ask if she'd be interested in swapping daughters with me."

Jenna's jaw dropped as she faked being insulted. "No way am I going along with this unless Annie's mom can prove there is a pool included in this offer. And I must have my own room, with a TV. Those are my terms. Ten bucks says her cooking's better than yours, anyway."

I raised an eyebrow at Jenna's mom, unsure. "There's a pool, and the cooking's not bad."

"Call me Nancy," she said breezily. "And don't worry, we're just teasing. If you only knew how many times I've tried to pawn this one off on some other unsuspecting family...but alas, it never works."

Jenna and her mom shared a private wink, and I felt a pang of jealousy. I had also never had the mom of a friend ask me to call her by her first name. Usually the adults I met were all about "respectful boundaries."

Looking away, I noticed Owen had inched closer to the window and was staring out, staring down into the street three floors below. It was too weird—like looking into a mirror. He was like me, the tag-along kid with a sibling in the hospital who had no real business being there. I wanted to say something to Owen, to tell him I understood his deal, but I couldn't think of anything except "Hi."

Owen looked up at me, alarmed.

Jenna spoke up. "You know how to play, right?" She was holding up a deck of cards. "Gin?"

I smiled at her. "Gin? No thanks, I'm trying to quit."

Nancy burst out laughing and Owen said "Laaaaaame."

Jenna rolled her eyes, smiling a sarcastic half-smile. "Oh that's a good one. Owen, will you bring that table and chairs over here?"

"Where's Amanda?" I asked as my eyes followed Owen and fell instead on the empty bed.

Jenna looked over at Amanda's empty bed too. "This is her chemo day. She'll be on the fourth floor all day and will come in sometime late tonight. Leukemia, you know. She's a bear right after a treatment."

So that explained the baldness. Poor Amanda.

Me, Owen, and Nancy each took seats at the table pushed up against Jenna's bed.

"So Annie, what—" Nancy began while Owen shuffled and dealt the cards.

"I'm here because of my brother," I blurted out automatically. "He had a brain tumor."

Nancy looked a little surprised.

Owen and Jenna froze.

"I'm sorry," Nancy said uncertainly. "I wasn't about to pounce…was just going to ask what types of things you're into besides card sharking."

"Ha!" Jenna erupted.

My voice came out as a mouse squeak, and I felt my cheeks get warm. "Sorry. I'm used to people asking about what's going on with my brother."

The cool skin of Nancy's hand on mine silenced me. "I know. But he's no doubt in good hands with lots of nurses fussing over him, and you're worth asking about, too."

I could tell she meant it, and it wasn't just something she was saying to be nice. I smiled at her gratefully and picked up my cards, taking a deep breath and giving her an edited variation of the bullet-point rundown I'd given Jenna. "I like cats, I dance, I like to journal, also I'm a pastor's daughter who's routinely running from the law… that type of thing."

Nancy was still smiling at me, her eyes quiet. "I like you," she said resolutely, picking up her cards and tapping them on the table, with a quick nod to Jenna. "I like her."

"Well," said Jenna coolly, struggling to arrange her cards with her one good hand and the side of her cast, "I already claimed her, so you can just find someone else to adopt and publicly embarrass."

Owen shook his head slowly, eyes on the ceiling. "Can we play, already?"

I didn't think of my own family again until I saw it was completely dark outside. As I said my goodbyes and rushed down the corridor, I saw Dad leave Daniel's room and walk slowly toward me. His eyes didn't register any surprise I'd materialized there after being gone for what must've been hours.

"Come on, kiddo, let's go," Dad said. "Tracy already left, she's having dinner with some friends tonight."

Lucky Tracy. But wait—lucky me, too! I felt like I had a secret. Like maybe even a whole secret other family.

Chapter 13

The next day at school, I was pleased to find I'd gotten an A on my history test. This was in addition to the A+ on my math pop quiz, just like Rachel predicted. I felt like I had a newly discovered and verified superpower. *Annie Spencer...good at school!*

At lunchtime I was more than happy to bask in the noise of my friends talking about anything that didn't involve hospitals. At church on Sunday I had already filled Rachel in on the latest news with Daniel's stroke and recovery, but I left out the part about my new friend at the hospital. She was deeply sympathetic at how long this was all dragging out, and I think she also understood I wanted school to be a place where we didn't have to talk about my family all the time.

After school I walked home and found Dad waiting for me so we could go to the hospital. I triumphantly handed him the tests I'd clutched all the way home. "Hey Dad, check it out!"

He smiled and glanced at the math quiz on top. "Daniel has always been so good at math. I hope the stroke hasn't affected that."

I deflated as he handed the papers back and smiled a sad smile at me. We got in the car, and I suddenly felt like I'd much rather tag along to Tracy's choir practice than be headed back to the hospital, Jenna or no Jenna.

When we arrived on Daniel's floor, we found him slowly making his way up the hallway with the aid of a hospital worker and a walker. I tried to keep the shock from registering on my face. He looked small but determined to take step after ponderous step. When he looked up at me I gave him a thumbs-up. He smiled his halfway smile at me, trying to raise his left hand in a wave. He looked exhausted. Dad and I watched him shuffle by, and the hospital worker told us brightly, "We're going to walk all the way to Daniel's therapy appointment!"

Dad began to follow them, and I motioned toward the waiting room, raising my backpack. He nodded, and with a small wave they were off. Hospital shorthand.

When I got to Jenna's door I found it closed, which meant only one thing: Amanda was there. I think she always insisted on keeping the door closed because she didn't like the people passing by to look at her. Just a guess, though. That's probably how I'd feel if I were her.

I knocked on the door and opened it, finding Jenna and Amanda but no Owen and no Nancy. Amanda greeted me with her trademark scowl, but Jenna's face lit up when I walked into the room.

"Hi! I've been so bored today. Get over here and keep me company."

Amanda looked instantly indignant. "Oh—what? What's that supposed to mean?"

Jenna turned to look at her. "Well, if you'd answer me when I talk to you, I'd consider you to be better company." She added a quiet "Maybe" at the end so only I could hear. We shared a conspiratorial glance as Amanda crossed her arms and scowled harder.

"Fine, I'll answer your question," Amanda spat. "You want to know how I'm feeling today? I feel horrible. And you can't know what that's like, because you and I are in two totally different worlds here."

Amanda's face had turned so red that her whole head looked like it belonged in a giant game of pool. Jenna and I looked at each other, shocked, as she continued. "Don't pretend like you don't know what I mean. Look at you—there's nothing *really* wrong with you, you're a healthy person who got injured. But me? I'm a sick person who will always be sick, and is sick in a way that it's part of who they are. I am a sick person, and you are a healthy person. That's why I don't answer when you ask how I'm feeling. Because even if I tried to tell you, you couldn't understand what my pain is like."

Jenna and I sat in stunned silence watching Amanda as her breathing slowed, her head returned to its normal color, and she slowly powered down from her outburst. I thought about Daniel—the old Daniel before the surgeries—and how he'd thought of himself as "A healthy person who got injured." He never considered himself one of the "really sick ones," but he was. I wondered if he still thought he wasn't.

Her face completely calm, Jenna moved her hand to her side and began to slowly un-snap her hospital gown to reveal the side of her stomach facing Amanda. There was a large white patch of gauze there, and as Jenna peeled it back I couldn't help but gasp. "Amanda, dear, if you wouldn't mind repeating that—" I watched as Amanda's head turned in slow motion. She was a goner.

"—I don't believe Bob could properly hear your speech under all these bandages."

Amanda's eyes locked onto Bob for a split-second as Jenna let out a whooping laugh so loud I thought for sure the nurses would come running.

"Grow up," Amanda grumbled. She turned her back to us and lay still while Jenna laughed.

I stared at Jenna's wound. It was like something off one of those hospital shows. There was a mess of staples chasing the cut up and down Jenna's side so it all looked like a miniature set of train tracks gone crazy. I tried not to think what must've happened to Jenna for a boat propeller to cause that kind of damage. Jenna stopped laughing when she saw my face, and there was silence.

She reached for the gauzy covering and I said the only thing I could think of. "You are one part paper doll, one part hummingbird, and one part Frankenstein. I believe you might be an endangered species."

Jenna paused, then smiled. "You've got that right."

I settled into the nearest chair and dumped my backpack on the floor. "Seriously though, that looks brutal. How do you deal with being in bed all day?"

"It's not the best time of my life. Just being honest. I have dreams where I get up out of this bed and run straight out of here. But I think that's a long way off."

"Maybe, maybe not." I replied. "My brother is actually starting to walk again. You might see him shuffle by here every once in a while. It's...actually a pretty depressing sight." I chuckled ruefully, but clapped a hand over my mouth. "Sorry, I know that's so bad to say."

But Jenna reassured me. "No, it's completely fine to say. It's the truth. It's your experience. I wish Owen would open up about what he's going through. I know it can't be easy hanging around this *amazing* place all the time." She gestured grandly around the room with her one good arm. "Lifestyles of the sad and bedridden."

A bag of chips came sailing over from Amanda's side of the room and hit Jenna squarely in the face. A laugh burst straight out of me.

"So am I the sad one, or the bedridden one?" Amanda spat.

"Thanks for the chips!" Jenna sang. "And who says I was talking about you? Anyway, sad is a choice. Bedridden is a fact. That's all I'm saying."

Chapter 14

I t took almost two weeks after Daniel's second surgery for him to start getting that mischievous glimmer back in his eyes. He was moved out of the ICU back to the children's floor, where he was a favorite among the nursing staff and his newly acquired army of physical therapists. I could see why they all liked him so much. One day I walked in to find Daniel's swollen face and lopsided smile were enhanced by several tongue depressors wedged into the staples holding his head together. It was quite a sight to behold, the question-mark-shaped scar dwarfed by the makeshift wooden mohawk served up some significant shock value. Leave it to Daniel to make an entertainer out of himself while he was semi-paralyzed in a hospital bed.

Not that things were usually fun like that. It was clear life was a struggle for Daniel, with new obstacles every day. Sometimes I would walk into Daniel's hospital room to find him sleeping and Mom crying, and when I'd tip-toe over to her she'd grab on and hold tight like something bad would happen if she didn't. And I never knew what to say. I wanted to ask her if she still believed in God the same way, or if she ever got scared things were never going to be like they were before. It was shocking seeing her like that, and I didn't want to make things worse, so mostly I stayed quiet.

Within a week of Daniel leaving the ICU Jenna was transferred out of the ICU too, and her new room was on the floor below Daniel's. She had the room to herself; Amanda had been moved out before Jenna and wasn't her roommate anymore. I thought about tracking Amanda down, but thinking about seeing her scowling face usually drove that urge away.

I saw Nancy all the time now. She was at the hospital whenever I was there, either in Jenna's room or down in the cafeteria to get some work done and make phone calls while Jenna slept. Sometimes after I'd stopped by Daniel's room and also checked up on Jenna, Nancy and I would stroll around the hospital together. She always said I was allowed to ask her anything I wanted, and I got brave some days. One day Nancy had a real craving for ice cream, so we went down to the cafeteria. When she'd gotten her coffee ice cream and I sat down with my mint chocolate chip, I asked her about Jenna and Owen's dad.

Nancy smiled sadly and sunk her plastic spoon deep into her ice cream. "He left us. About ten years ago when Jenna and Owen were four. He said he didn't care for the family life."

"Wow," was all I could say. I felt instantly bad for asking about something so personal, but nothing about Nancy's appearance signaled she was offended or uncomfortable.

Actually, she started laughing. "I mean, right? Can you imagine turning your back on all *this*?" She made a sweeping gesture that included herself and the expanse of the hospital, and beyond that, what I could imagine was a home life packed with warmth, laughter, and getting to talk about whatever messy and complicated feelings you felt.

I cocked my head and watched her absorb a giant bite of ice cream. "I actually can't imagine why anyone would. You and your family are incredibly fun and amazing. You guys are the real deal, and anyone who doesn't see that is missing out, big time."

Nancy swallowed hard and blinked back sudden tears. "Ok, little miss," she laughed, dabbing her eyes. "You will stop that right now. I vowed not to cry in this hospital today."

I laughed and felt tears of my own spring up. "But it's so fun!"

And then there we were, laughing and crying right in the hospital cafeteria and I didn't care who saw.

"I wish I could talk to my parents like this," I confessed when we'd more or less gotten ahold of ourselves. "I feel so bad asking them how they're feeling or trying to explain how I feel. I'm always afraid of saying the wrong thing, and I don't want to make them cry even more so I just… don't ask."

Nancy nodded, smiling her sad, reassuring smile she wears when I talk about my family. "Don't worry, you'll find a way. I know it takes a while for people to be able to talk about what hurts. It's especially tough to do when you're in the middle of it and not quite sure if things are going to turn out how you want them to. But sometimes the pain we feel is the most genuine thing about us that we can share with other people—so why hide it?"

I nodded slowly, letting that sink in. "Owen can ask you anything about what's going on, and I think that helps."

Nancy smiled. "I hope so. But you know, he doesn't tend to take advantage of that too often. Not even on our Tuesday nights."

"What are your Tuesday nights?" I felt a wistful stab remembering my former life of Tuesdays spent babysitting with Rachel.

Nancy leaned in and whispered, "Promise not to tell a soul?"

I grinned at her and matched her hushed tones, like we were spies. "Depends. Does Jenna count?"

She rolled her eyes, then mouthed, "Owen and his mother go on dates together every Tuesday night."

I sat back in my chair. "Dates?"

"Shhhhh!" she hissed, eyes wide. After an exaggerated scan of the cafeteria to make sure we hadn't been overheard, she continued in a murmur. "Yes, dates. We'll go to dinner, catch a movie, sometimes just walk around the block a few times. It's our chance to catch up and I always look forward to it. And Owen, sometimes he doesn't even mind putting in the face time with this here old lady."

She winked and I laughed. If there was one thing Nancy wasn't, it was old. Her features always looked fresh to me, untouched by the worry that was everywhere else in my world.

I mashed my remaining ice cream against the inside of the paper cup. "What do you guys talk about?"

"Oh, everything." She smiled brightly, but it quickly faded. "Except…things have been different since Jenna's accident. He doesn't like to talk about it, and I don't force him to."

I nodded.

Nancy continued, a faraway look on her face. "It's like with visiting her here, I guess. I always ask him if he wants to come with me. Life's too short for telling people they *should* do something or they *need* to do something. And I know my kid. If I tell him he's got to be here, he'll grow to resent me for it. But if he decides on his own he wants to be here, at least it was his decision."

Decision. The word had more weight than the others, and I thought about it. It wasn't much of a decision for me to come here to the hospital. I came home from school and then I came here, most days. Or if Dad wasn't home, someone from church always showed up to cart me off. These days Tracy had a pretty steady routine of practices, work, time with friends, and track meets, and she popped by the hospital when she could. And it was just what we all did. I didn't ask why, and nobody asked if I actually wanted to go or not.

I avoided Nancy's eyes. "You know, if someone had asked me, I probably would've decided to come anyway. But it would've felt better if it were my decision to be here all the time."

She smiled the sad smile again. The smile that says *This won't be how it is forever* and *I know it's not fun, and I'm sorry.*

We sat and it was quiet, but not uncomfortable.

After a few minutes had gone by, her quiet voice nudged into my thoughts. "Do you think I'm doing a passable job with Owen? Sometimes I look at him and he's so sad it breaks my heart. I'm doing the best I can, but it doesn't feel like enough sometimes." Her face was so vulnerable I wanted to look away. Moms weren't supposed to say stuff like this to kids, were they? Didn't it break some sort of rule?

"I think you're doing great, but what do I know?"

"You know more than you think, kid. You're living it too."

I shrugged. "That's true, I guess."

I thought of how the hospital always felt lonely and overwhelming to me, in the days before I'd met Jenna. How I used to spend hours in Daniel's hospital room, curled up in the corner trying to stay out of the way because I couldn't make things better, or else I'd wander the hospital like some kind of lost puppy.

"I think he doesn't like the way this place makes him feel," I told Nancy, images flashing in my mind of Owen, quiet in Jenna's room. Owen by the window looking down, his face so gray and drawn. "He's sad. Just like me," it came out in a whisper.

It was quiet again, and then Nancy spoke. "He used to stay at home and barely come to the hospital at all. Now at least he comes sometimes…I think it's because of you." She waggled her eyebrows and I burned an imaginary hole staring through my empty ice cream cup, willing myself not to blush. I could sense her restraining herself from nudging me with her elbow. "So how can I help him not be so sad?"

I thought for a second before answering. It was simple, really. But I'll bet it made all the difference. "Never stop the dates."

Chapter 15

Tracy came home after midnight. She'd had a track meet and I wondered how it had gone. Right when I heard her footsteps pass by my door, I faked a cough. Loudly. Tracy's footsteps stopped, backtracked, and she flicked on the lights.

I slammed my pillow over my face in mock outrage. "Hey, what's the big idea? Can't a girl get some sleep?"

Tracy laughed sarcastically. "Oh stop, drama queen."

I peeked out from under my pillow as she dropped her track bag on the floor in a defeated heap. The silver and blue ribbons in her hair hung limp and uneven, and she looked tired. Smokey, offended at having been awakened, stretched and hopped off the bed. Tracy nudged him with her foot as he stalked by.

"How was your meet?" I asked, knowing already from her demeanor that the news probably wasn't good.

She stretched out her arms and flopped across the foot of my bed, turning her head to look over at me. "No guts, no glory. I just don't feel like running these days. It's not as much fun knowing Dad isn't in the bleachers recording the race, and Mom isn't there with her bag of dehydrated banana slices. And you're not there with a book, and Daniel's not there making up weird cheers."

I blinked at her. "We're sorry. Your meets are boring, and we are important people."

Tracy laughed so hard I thought she was going to wake up Dad. I threw my pillow at her and thought about how when nobody came to my dance recital, I certainly hadn't felt like laughing.

Tracy's laughter trailed off. She shook her head and stood up with a groan. Scooping up her track bag, she headed to the door.

She paused when I spoke. "It's going to get better, right? Things will be normal again someday?"

"What even does *normal* mean, anyway? If you thought our family was ever some shade of normal, I've got some bad news."

I caught the pillow she tossed back. "I guess you've got me there. But have you thought about what it's going to be like when Daniel comes home? What if he never gets back to where he was? Do you think he knows what he's lost?"

The light in Tracy's eyes faded, and I felt guilty for peppering her with every worry on my mind the second she stepped in the door.

But she took a deep breath and replied anyway. "For his sake, I hope he doesn't realize what he's lost. It's hard to tell right now what things will be like when he eventually comes home, but it's safe to say things are going to be different from now on. And we should all start accepting that."

Chapter 16

The next day at school I was dragging. I trudged into my English class in a fog of thoughts about what things would be like when Daniel came home—whenever *that* was. It was something I was feeling more anxious about as the days slid by with only minor glimmers of recovery.

"Ok, everyone," Mr. Maher said after the bell rang, "your writing prompt for the day is here on the board. You know the rules… start writing and don't stop. You have fifteen minutes to wow me—and GO!"

I looked up to see *Colors: How do you see the world?* written on the board, and thought about my family and how what we were going through was changing each of us. These days Dad looked like he was carrying the weight of the world, and Mom's broken heart was perpetually displayed on her face. Even Tracy's light seemed dimmer these days, and me? I was a ping-pong ball constantly smacked between the sadness of my family and my hopes that someday, somehow, things would be better than they were right now. I got out a piece of paper and the words tumbled out.

> I used to see life as the tranquil, clear ocean blue of "I know who I am" and the spring meadow green of "I belong here." But everything is different now because my brother had a brain tumor. Now I look around and see the quiet, deep ocean blue sadness of sitting by a window in a hospital room and disappearing a little more each day. And I see the muffled, dead-grass green pain that whispers "I don't belong here." My colors aren't bright enough anymore for anybody to see unless they take the time to look really closely.

> My brother Daniel used to see life in exciting yellows and oranges, harmless colors that are fun and happy. Even when we all found out he had a brain tumor, I watched Daniel take that scary, weird information and turn it into a sunshine-colored surprise vacation from school and a bright orange chance to go somewhere new and experience something different. But then he had an operation, and another one, and a stroke. After that, I could tell his colors were swirling into a dull winter sun yellow that asks "How come I can't walk

anymore?" and an orange that's burnt at the edges by new words like "limitation" and also "might be semi-permanent" and "visual blind spots." But still, Daniel keeps on smiling his yellow and orange smile the best he can. His colors are muted now but they are still his colors.

My sister Tracy's colors are eggplant purple responsibility, and a lavender-tinted need to take care of things, to keep our family together and happy. But I can tell she's sad, too, underneath it all. And her once-vibrant purple is more like a bruised plum that pleads "How can I make this better? Nothing can make this better."

My parents used to have all kinds of colors, but right now they can only see the blood-red that screams "Emergency!" and "Urgent!" and "Right now this is what is most important to us!" And when your vision is flooded with red, you can't see much else and I guess it's not your fault. But that doesn't mean there aren't other things to see. Things that you are missing.

Honestly, I'm starting to hate the colors. I wish we could all see each other clearly and see everything else around us, without the colors getting in the way.

"Time's up!" Mr. Maher called out from the back of the room. As he strode up the aisle, I felt two fat tears slide down my cheeks and make an unmistakable *splat* on my paper right as he passed by. Whoops.

He stopped, held out his hand for my paper, and when I glanced up he was looking straight over his glasses into my teary eyes. I saw both compassion and quiet pride in his expression as he whispered "Congratulations, Annie. You're a real writer now."

With a small smile I quickly wiped away the "real writer" evidence on my face. It didn't look like anyone else had seen my embarrassing display. The rest of the time we got to spend reading silently, and when the bell rang, Mr. Maher called me over to his desk. *So much for keeping school a tumor-free zone*, I thought.

My writing prompt was sitting there smack-dab in the middle of his desk. He looked at it, and looked at me. A pause, like he was deciding what to say. "When I was in high school I had this football coach, and he said something I'll never forget. He told me that to find the best players, you have to look for the ones who can give it their all, even when they're hurting. The ones who can play through the pain."

Another pause, but I couldn't meet his eyes.

He continued. "I imagine it's been difficult to deal with school while there's so much going on at home. But your teachers all know about your family's situation, and we see how hard you're working. We're proud of how you're playing through the pain."

Speechless, I managed a weak, tearful smile at Mr. Maher's shoe.

He held up my paper. "As for this, I'm afraid you're not getting it back. I'm submitting it to the district writing contest and I hope you win."

I let out a surprised laugh and heard myself blurt out "For real? But there are tears on it." I wiped away the new tears that had sprung up, uninvited. There was too much to process. I felt like I'd been hiding on a dark stage but then *bam* someone turned on the spotlight.

"Tears and all. Now scoot on out, or you'll miss your lunchtime."

"Thank you," I managed to choke out before scurrying away.

The rest of the day I was floating ten feet off the ground. Nothing could touch me. In my afternoon classes I secretly studied each teacher's face. Did they really know about Daniel's tumor? Had they known all along? Maybe it was my imagination, but Madame Kaessler sure gave me the best spot while we were blocking out our new group routine. And my history teacher for sure doesn't have a good poker face, turns out. When I took the time to notice, I saw how tenderly she met my eyes when I sat down, and the little wink as I walked out after class. Then there was sixth period science, which was not what I'd typically consider a fun and nurturing experience. Except, had Mr. Claridge ever beamed quite like that when I'd volunteered an answer before? And did he definitely put me with the smartest kids for our group project?

Maybe at the beginning of this whole tumor ordeal I would've felt embarrassed and overwhelmed by all the attention. But now I truly appreciated it.

Chapter 17

The next time I was at the hospital I tried a little experiment. Instead of making a beeline for Daniel's room with my eyes glued to the floor, I paid attention. I met every eye and returned every smile. And what I found was this: I was not as invisible as I thought I was.

When I got to Daniel's room I noticed the crisp autumn breeze sailing through an open window, reminding me Halloween was coming up and it was time to replenish the stash of pumpkin Peeps. And there was Daniel in his hospital-issued wheelchair, left arm clad in a brace keeping his hand open, and left ankle in a brace that kept his foot from dragging. And he was grinning away, with a little more orange and yellow in his smile than I remembered. Things were looking up!

Jenna's recovery was a different situation altogether, with her doctor giving her broken limbs X-rays to see whether she was healed enough for the casts to come off. She wasn't. The gash in her side also didn't appear to be getting much better. Although Jenna would never let on how much pain she was in, I could tell her long hospital stay was taking a toll on her. Her eyes had a little less sparkle every time I saw her, and Nancy's face wore uncharacteristic worry as she stroked Jenna's hair when she was too uncomfortable to sleep.

Still, I looked at Nancy with new eyes and saw her color was the royal blue of bravery and strength. She believed life was full of challenges that were meant to be faced, not hidden from. Royal blue people didn't make excuses or blame others, or wait for someone else to take care of them. It was the strongest color I knew.

Our whole family spent Halloween at the hospital, which was pretty much as strange as it sounds. Daniel convinced one of his nurses to let him raid the floor's medical supplies, and next thing I knew he was swaddled head to toe in gauze with his arms outstretched.

"I'm a mummy!" Daniel squealed, staggering around his hospital room and momentarily tripping over his cane.

As for the rest of us, Tracy blew up several surgical gloves and tied them off, attaching a pair of each with bobby pins to our heads so they stood up like antlers. She rummaged in her purse to find black eyeliner and bright red lipstick, and joyfully painted a dainty black reindeer nose on a slightly reluctant Mom and Dad, then herself.

Who do you think got to be Rudolph with the bright red lipstick nose? I tried to take it as a compliment.

We all traipsed down the hall in a slow-moving clump, chorusing "Trick or treat!" at each nurses' station. Mom fussed endlessly over Daniel's ever-loosening gauze trail that threatened to derail us all. Several nurses and other patients were dressed up and stalking the halls, an assortment of wheelchairs, IV poles, and bandaged wounds that might not have been part of a costume. "Monster Mash" played in a crackling loop over the intercom. It was the world's most depressing parade.

I glanced at Tracy, who somehow even looked pretty dressed as a surgical glove reindeer. "This is like a dream I had once. And not a good one."

She threw back her head and laughed, glove antlers bobbing, and tossed a miniature box of Dots my way. "I already looked, these are all yellows."

"Everyone knows yellow is the worst flavor of any candy," I said, but I ate them anyway.

I snuck a picture of all of us and texted it to Jenna. *For an article I'm writing: A Fashionista's Guide to a Fab-boo-lous Hospital Halloween!*

Jenna instantly put a "Haha" reaction on the photo, then wrote back, *From drab to fab! Don't let that bleeding head wound cramp your style—accessorize!*

I sent an obnoxious amount of hysterical laughter emojis, to which she responded, *Please don't leave tonight without letting me mock you for that costume in person.*

—m—

It wasn't even a week later that I came home from school to find Dad home, talking excitedly into his phone. He hung up a few minutes later and rushed down the hall into my room.

"Daniel's coming home! The doctors say he's healed enough, and he can continue most of his physical therapy here!" Dad was positively radioactive with joy.

My heart lifted. Finally—no more living at the hospital.

"That's great!" I smiled a real smile. It felt like forever since our whole family had been in the house at the same time. Maybe now everything would start to return to normal—I couldn't wait. Plus, this meant Mom and Daniel would be home for the holidays! Judging by the Halloween debacle, I hadn't been keen to witness the hospital's take on Thanksgiving and Christmas celebrations.

Daniel gets to come home from the hospital!! I texted Jenna first, then Rachel.

FINALLY! came Rachel's reply less than a minute later.

Good! I'm going to hitch a ride and bust out of here, too, came Jenna's text later that night.

I'll stock up on sugar packets… I replied with a vomit emoji and a pink heart.

Chapter 18

Daniel and Mom made their grand homecoming the very next day, and it took an additional trip to the hospital to retrieve Daniel's gifts from his many well-wishers. Mom laughed as she struggled to get in the door with a fistful of get-well cards and drooping mylar balloons, and the banner from Daniel's fifth grade class rolled under her arm. "Would you believe we even left some of his balloons and flowers at the hospital for his nurses and the other kids?"

I reached out to hug my long-lost mom, and instead found my arms were embracing the bulk of her balloon and card load.

"Hi, Annie," she said. "There's more in the car. Would you mind?"

Not exactly the tearful reunion I'd pictured.

When I returned with the next load of trinkets, I found Daniel slowly making his way around the living room with the help of his cane. Lovingly, he touched the photos on the walls like he'd forgotten what the house looked like. Meanwhile, Mom wasted no time. She got the card table out and was in the process of organizing mounds of paper into different piles around it. Her own command center.

Dinner that night felt more than a little strange. Tracy was picking up a dinner shift at work so it was just the four of us, and still the table felt crowded. As good as it was to have Mom and Daniel home again, it wasn't quite like it used to be. For one thing, all of the conversation centered around the hospital. Also, Daniel had to use special silverware with a foam grip. We all watched him make the huge effort to grab his special fork, but his fingers didn't want to cooperate. He finally used his other hand to maneuver his left fingers around the fork and slowly, slowly scooped some mashed potatoes onto it.

Dad wore a tired smile, and Mom was the picture of grim determination. I guess I hadn't thought about how Daniel would need to re-learn things like how to use silverware.

Later on when Tracy came home, she gave Mom and Daniel each a huge hug. We all stood around for a while, not knowing what to do with ourselves. It was like we were all pieces of the same puzzle and we used to fit together, but now there was a new piece and we couldn't figure out how to make it fit. We settled on watching *The Nightmare Before Christmas* together, and I watched Mom get Daniel settled on the couch with a blanket.

She sat down next to him and reached for his left hand, massaging his palm and easing his fingers open. "His physical therapists told me it helps to loosen the tendons so he can stretch out his hand more."

Daniel met my eyes and gave me a weak smile. "Working my way back up to a high-five, I guess."

I smiled back. "You'll get there."

The next morning when I was getting ready to leave for school, I noticed some of the other changes. Mom and Daniel were already up, Mom rushing up and down the hallway grabbing records and X-rays for some kind of therapy visit they were going to. The house did feel fuller and more chaotic, but it was more than that. Looking around the kitchen, I saw that my dance photo from last year on the fridge had been covered up by a picture of Daniel and his team of physical therapists from the hospital. There was also the flyer for a place advertising outpatient physical therapy, prominently placed onto our family calendar.

I nearly collided with the card table on my way to the front door, watching as Mom rushed Daniel out, practically shutting the door in my face. No denying it, Tracy had been right. Things were different.

"Good to have you home," I mumbled as I trudged out after them.

At school I was almost able to convince myself that life was at least on its way to being completely fine. My friends were overjoyed Daniel was home now, even though we didn't talk much about it these days. But when I got home from school that day, reality crashed through. Daniel was zonked out in front of the TV and Mom was sifting through a fresh batch of papers at her command center.

I approached her table. "Hey, what's all that?"

She looked up at me and rolled her eyes. "Papers from the insurance company and more hospital bills. What a mess. I guess this is my job now, eh?"

I thought she meant it as a joke, but I didn't think it was funny. It was pretty accurate. She'd now have to be a mom second, and recovery drill sergeant, insurance bulldog, and therapy coordinator first.

I caught sight of one of the hospital bills and the $130,000 total at the bottom. I gasped. "That's how much it costs to get a brain tumor out??"

Mom glanced up at me and offered a weak laugh. "Oh, that's not even the half of it. But insurance will cover the majority—at least, that's the plan."

Wow.

I looked around the room at all of the new things that had materialized overnight. A therapy ball in the corner, posters on the wall for Daniel's vision exercises, and a stretchy strap attached to a doorknob. I felt silly for ever believing that once Daniel came home everything would be like it was before. I knew the whole situation wasn't his fault, but it was still annoying to have a house filled with reminders of his ordeal. It felt like it was beginning to define our entire family.

As for Daniel himself, now that he was home, the full scope of what he'd lost was coming into focus. In some ways he seemed like the same happy, goofy kid he was before. He still sang little nonsense songs to himself and played hide and seek with Smokey. And then I'd see him struggle to walk down the hall, left arm slumped and left leg trailing. Daniel didn't seem so normal then, and in other ways I was beginning to see the differences that might last his entire life.

The doctors told us Daniel's visual blind spots were most likely permanent. They had mapped out his whole visual field during his hospital stay, and found ten-inch splotches of blank space now existed on his left side, right around the center. Around the house it was easy enough for him to get around, if he went slow. But when he was in a new place it was a whole different story. Once, when he and I went with Mom to the grocery store, Daniel fully walked into a temporary display of chips like it wasn't even there. The wire shelving tipped over with a deafening clatter, and bags of chips flew everywhere. Other shoppers stopped to stare. Daniel was stunned, and Mom spoke in hushed tones to the store workers who scurried over to help us round up the chip bags from the floor. I watched the whole scene unfold in slow motion, and as I snatched up chip bags all I could think about was the inevitable day when a teenage Daniel would have friends who were all learning to drive. Would he be able to do that too? Did he think about things like that?

That was the thing about Daniel, though. He seemed to take all of the changes in stride, and not dwell too much on how things used to be. He'd just calmly go about his business, slower than before but as if things had always been this way. If it were me, I'd probably spend my days sobbing into my pillow at the unfairness of it all.

Not that Daniel was some angel who cooperated all of the time. I witnessed more than one episode of therapy exercises when Daniel hit a wall and refused to continue. Mom was always at his side urging him to "Supinate, now pronate." That meant he was supposed to practice using his left wrist to move his hand around. From what I could tell, *supinate* was turning your hand so the palm faced up, and *pronate* was where you turned your wrist so the palm faced down. It was difficult for him to do, by the looks of things. And I tried not to watch him struggle to raise his left thumb in the thumbs-up position Mom had been working with him on. When he'd had enough one day, he sat there looking like a blank version of stubborn, and eventually Mom gave up too.

It was just me and Daniel sitting on the couch in front of an episode of *The Simpsons*.

He sighed, and spoke without looking at me. "I know it doesn't make sense, but part of me really thought my paralysis only existed at the hospital. Like once I came home, I would be all better."

I glanced at him sideways, and when he looked back at me there it all was. The memory that life had not always been this tough…a twinge of jealousy and maybe wishing we could switch places. I could definitely beat him in Mario Kart now and maybe he knew that too, and then the look was gone.

As if he hadn't been through enough already, Daniel also had a giant pile of schoolwork to catch up on. He used to breeze through school, but things were different now. Even with Mom holding the pencil, Daniel struggled to remember things he used to know by heart. The math skills that had been his signature trait were just a memory now. He lost patience with the spelling words he definitely would've known before.

"Is it because of the stroke?" Tracy asked Mom, out of Daniel's earshot.

Mom looked at her sadly, and nodded. "Yes. It has something to do with memory and cognitive functioning. The doctors say math is specifically challenging for some stroke victims."

Tracy frowned. "That hardly seems fair, considering everything else he's lost."

Mom sighed. "Don't I know it."

Chapter 19

D aniel and Mom didn't come to church the first couple of Sundays they were home. I think facing everyone full force was a little intimidating for Daniel, but Dad still talked about Daniel in those sermons, just like almost every sermon nowadays. Mostly he'd marvel at how optimistic and trusting Daniel was, and I could feel several pairs of eyes on me. It felt overwhelming, mostly because I wasn't sure how people expected me to react. Were they waiting for me to jump up and shout "AMEN"?

Daniel's first Sunday back was a huge deal. Everybody was excited and wanted to talk to him, lining up to give him and my mom big hugs and exuberant well-wishes. I watched from the sidelines as Daniel absorbed it all, seeming absolutely delighted. But soon his shoulders sagged and he labored to drag his braced left foot along. His face still looked halfway slackened from his stroke, and after answering the same questions forty-five times the light had gone out of his eyes.

We all sat down as the service began—I sat with Mom and Daniel because Rachel's parents had a perfect sense of timing and decided to camp in Yellowstone right when I needed Rachel most.

Mom whispered to me as I sat down, "Daniel actually needs to sit there so I can massage his hand."

With a twinge of annoyance I shuffled over. As we all got settled it felt like everyone in the entire place was staring at us. It didn't feel nice, but I tried to remember this big group of people wasn't some overwhelming mob—it was made up of individuals. Some had taken time out of their day to drive me to the hospital, some had brought meals, some had sent cards and letters and gifts. Odds were, everyone in that room had also offered sincere prayers on our family's behalf. It helped to think of it that way, but still, I looked forward to the attention dying down. It had to end eventually, right?

I missed Rachel. She would have understood how awkward and intense this felt. Tracy was singing up front, and she didn't appear bothered by the uptick in attention. Dad's sermon was sprinkled generously with references to Daniel, and to my shock and amazement Daniel actually looked a little embarrassed by the whole thing. He stared at the carpet and repeatedly scuffed the toe of his right shoe lightly against the chair leg in front of him. He tried to shift down into his seat, but Mom propped him back up.

When the service was winding down, Dad wrapped things up with a reminder that there was going to be a reception held after services to thank everyone for their help and to celebrate Daniel coming home. Everyone clapped, and Daniel blushed.

Mom caught my eye over Daniel's head. "Would you mind getting his arm brace from the car?"

I gave a quick nod. I was glad to have something to do besides stand there as the extra kid who nodded and smiled over and over as each person said the exact same thing: "I'll bet it's wonderful having Daniel home again!"

I took my time retrieving Daniel's brace, and on my way back Travis fell into step next to me. "Hey."

I saluted with Daniel's arm brace and Travis laughed, rolling his eyes. "I'm surprised you're not already hiding out somewhere. It's a madhouse today."

"Yeah, it's pretty intense. I don't know what to do with myself, honestly."

Travis smiled sympathetically and stopped walking, turning toward me. "It must feel weird. But I want you to know lots of people understand this situation is hard for you, too. That Tracy is old enough to handle everything but you sometimes get left behind in the fray."

Well, this was news. "Wow—thanks. It's been a lot. The sermons especially."

Travis nodded slowly. "Yeah, I can see that. Your brother's in a tough situation and your whole family is going through something most people never have to experience. It's a huge deal for you all. I can see how all the weirdness and attention could wear you out after a while, but it's also true Daniel needs help and attention and care in ways most people wouldn't."

I think this was the most Travis had ever said to me all at once, and he seemed to sense that I noticed. "I'm sorry if that sounded preachy. Just wanted to say people do understand what you're feeling, and that you're feeling it for plenty of justified reasons."

I nodded and looked at him, puzzled. "Why even bother to tell me all this?"

He laughed. "Well, to be perfectly honest, you *are* way less annoying like this. I haven't really missed the ridiculously embarrassing flirting."

What?

"But in all seriousness, you're hurting and I don't like to see that. I've known you a long time and I consider you to be my friend. Friends help each other out when they're hurting."

"Yes, they do," I said with a smile. I silently assigned Travis the color gunmetal gray. Something steady and strong hid below the surface, but there were brilliant flashes of something electric there too—when he decided to share them. "I hear you, and I appreciate the pep talk."

He opened the door for me. "Right. Anytime."

As I walked back into the sanctuary to deliver Daniel's brace, I saw lots of beaming faces turn toward me. Everything in me wanted to shrink back, to run away, but instead I stood tall. In those faces I saw something new…the radiant, gleaming gold light that said "We love you. You're going to be okay. And we will be here, always."

Chapter 20

I started to see the colors absolutely everywhere. The buoyant, steadily cheerful teal of Rachel's encouraging presence at school that never forced me to talk about Daniel. The unmistakable warm bronze beams radiating toward me from my teachers. I also got to see the steely, strong silver determination that said "I know you can do it" from Daniel's physical therapists.

Now that Daniel was released from the hospital, he only had to go back once a week for physical therapy. Part of me couldn't believe I was now asking to tag along to the hospital, but I missed Jenna and Nancy. Even Owen.

I texted Jenna throughout the week, but it wasn't the same as sitting there for hours with her and her family, free to be me and feel whatever I was feeling that day. Mom never questioned me directly about why on earth I was so eager to waltz back into the hospital time after time. I guess I could see why she wouldn't. Besides taking Daniel there for his therapy sessions, I knew she used the time to catch up with a few of the nurses, doctors, and even janitorial staff who had stuck close during this crisis and become a second family. They were a new network, a crucial support for an area of life she never thought she'd have to tread, much less with her baby boy. I think she understood on some level that she wasn't the only one who had made friends there. The hospital had become a part of all of our lives, like it or not.

Thanksgiving was upon us out of nowhere, and along with it came my report card. Straight A's! That was a first for me. I guess all my hard work had paid off, and I was beyond thrilled. The first thing I did was stroll up to Mom and place it right on top of the pile of paperwork she was peering a hole into. She picked up the report card, studied it, and smiled. She was proud of me! Maybe she would show my grandparents when they came over for Thanksgiving dinner.

This year we were having a quiet gathering with just my grandparents coming over. They gave Daniel a huge squeeze right when they walked in the door, and all during dinner the conversation revolved around Daniel's recovery. I hoped the topic would turn to something else. *"Annie got straight A's!"* Mom would say, beaming at me. But alas, no mention came. Maybe she'd forgotten. It was hard not to sulk as I cleared the dishes.

In the living room Grandma found a Hallmark

Christmas movie and cranked the volume up. Mom was in the kitchen putting away leftovers, and the others had migrated over to the prized possession of the Spencer home—the foosball table Dad had found at a garage sale for twenty bucks. Its glassy surface was cracked a bit in the middle and one of the legs had to be propped up with cardboard to make the table level, but nobody ever minded. Least of all Daniel, who had been perfecting a one-handed playing strategy. I had to give him points for effort there.

I approached Mom after clearing away all the dishes and wiping off the table. "Why didn't you mention my grades at dinner?" It came out as a whimper, unfortunately.

Mom had started washing the giant pile of dirty dishes, and she sighed without looking at me. "Daniel's report card was pretty rough. He's behind but he's trying. I didn't want to make him feel bad by mentioning your grades."

"Oh, wow." Who would give bad grades to a kid who just had a brain tumor and a stroke? Part of me wanted to feel indignant at the injustice of it all...too bad there wasn't much room for compassion in my heart tonight. Were his grades my fault? No. "Does that mean I should feel bad for getting good grades, though? I worked so hard and you're acting like it's something to be hidden."

Mom didn't say anything or turn around, just kept right on washing those dishes as if it were the only normal activity left in her life and she had to cling to it. In a flash,

I understood the situation perfectly. There had been no mention of my report card because I was the measuring stick now. The better I did, the more it reminded my parents about what Daniel had lost. It *was* something to be hidden, which wasn't fair, but that was the reality for now. It was completely no-win for me. Crushed, I backed out of the kitchen and joined Grandma on the couch.

When she smiled and winked at me with the rosy pink cheer that bubbled "Isn't this a great day?" I had to fight from crying right then and there. I simmered angrily in the realization that I didn't have my own identity anymore where Mom was concerned. I was a comparison to Daniel, and was only allowed to be as good at things as he was.

Chapter 21

The next week held the bracing new chill of December, but I still felt bothered as I tagged along to the hospital to visit Jenna. It stung every time I thought about how the news of my hard-earned grades had fizzled out before it even got started. What was the point of trying so hard if nobody noticed? Would my family ever notice anything I did from now on?

When we arrived I set out in the opposite direction as Mom and Daniel, and was startled to hear a voice behind me calling my name.

"Annie! Hey." A red-faced Owen jogged up to me. He seemed extremely nervous. "I was over by the lake and I saw you up ahead, so I thought I'd see if you wanted some company."

"I'm glad you did." I meant it.

He smiled and we started walking. "How was your Thanksgiving?"

"It was pretty good," I lied.

Owen nodded, unconvinced, but didn't press me.

I smiled politely at him. "How about you?"

"Pretty strange considering how Jenna and Mom were here…I went to my aunt and uncle's house and we had their traditional Thanksgiving turducken."

"What is a turducken?"

His eyes grew wide and he stopped in his tracks. "Are you being serious? You haven't ever had turducken?"

I laughed and shook my head.

Owen's eyes sparked to life. "You start with a turkey, see? And it has to be a big turkey because otherwise the proportions would be all off and you'd end up with way more of one thing than the other, like this *one* time when my uncle was cooking and—"

"Owen?" I interrupted.

"It's a chicken, stuffed in a duck, stuffed in a turkey."

I must've looked horrified, because he explained, "It's actually pretty good. I know it sounds like something a lunatic would come up with, but it's pretty common."

"You would actually claim that a food substance with *turd* in the name and which contains three animals mashed together is common? It sounds like a crime against nature to me. And I could've done without the explanatory hand gestures, also."

He grinned. For the first time since I'd met him, he looked completely relaxed and there was no sadness in his eyes. *This must be what the real Owen is like*, I thought as we walked along the sidewalk that led back to the lake.

Underneath all of the sadness, this is Owen. I also found myself thinking Owen was actually pretty cute, away from the hospital.

We walked around the lake twice and then went into the hospital to see Jenna, speculating about what other abominations one could create in the name of gourmet cooking. Owen claimed there was already such a thing as a bacon-wrapped Twinkie that was deep-fried and topped with whipped cream and chocolate sauce, but I had my doubts.

"It's true!" Owen protested. "I'll take you to the state fair someday and prove it."

When we stumbled laughing and rosy-cheeked into Jenna's room, she and Nancy looked at us and then at each other, smirking.

Owen narrowed his eyes at them. "What?"

"Nothing," Nancy sang, as Jenna laughed. It was good to hear her laugh again. "I just remembered I desperately need some Pepsi for Jenna. Would you two mind?"

Owen and I looked at each other and shrugged, doing an about-face from the room to walk right back down the hall. We were approaching Nora's desk when I stopped abruptly, pointing to where she sat. "Owen, check it out!"

"What?"

"The pen, of course! Look at Nora's pen."

Nora was using—actually *using*—this pen that clearly belonged on display somewhere. It had a blue aluminum shaft with a clear purple clicker on top, shaped like a brain.

The best part was that whenever she put the pen to paper, the purple plastic brain lit up. Truly a thing of beauty.

Owen laughed as he saw the ridiculous look of longing I knew must be on my face.

"Laugh if you want. But I make no excuses for my love of a good pen."

Owen shrugged. "I collect interesting Band-Aids. Umm, new ones. Not used."

"I hope so," I laughed, and Nora waved at us as we went on our way.

"So what makes for a great pen?" Owen asked once we were out of earshot.

I rolled up my sleeves. "Well, sir, I'd be happy to tell you. The truly fantastic ones don't come along too often. Every great pen has to have certain features…comfortable grip, satisfying *click* for click pens, interesting design, that type of thing. And of course, if it doesn't have a steady ink flow and nice color then it is not a pen, it is a stick."

Owen smiled. "You're weird."

I smiled back. "You collect Band-Aids."

We reached the first floor waiting room, which had the only soda machine with Pepsi in it. Owen put in some change and punched the Pepsi button, and we were on our way.

"What about you?" I asked him. "What makes Band-Aids any more collectible than pens?"

He smirked at me. "Clearly you've never had a bad experience with a Band-Aid. If you had, you'd learn to appreciate the great ones. They have to be flexible but not fall apart too easily, and they can't be too stiff in case you need them for a finger. The adhesive has to last through washing your hands, but can't leave sticky gunk on your skin. And if it has a great design or glows in the dark, it helps you heal faster. That's a fact."

I laughed and Owen beamed. "We're a match made in office supply heaven," I said.

Chapter 22

On Friday night Rachel invited our whole school crew to sleep over, and I was excited to get out of the house. It was strange to think about how different my friendship with my school friends was from my friendship with the Walkers. I'd never even hung out with Jenna outside of the hospital, but the Walkers all knew and understood more about what was going on in my life than I'd told any of my school friends, Rachel included.

I wondered what it would be like to introduce Rachel and Jenna. Would they get along? Maybe. I guess there was the chance Rachel could be grossed out by Jenna's injuries, and would she think it was all that funny to name your own cut? Then again, maybe they'd hit it off so well they'd like each other more than they liked me. That was an uncomfortable thought. I liked having them both to myself.

My mind snapped back to reality as Dad pulled the car up to Rachel's house. I walked in the door, greeted by the smell of cinnamon rolls wafting from the kitchen and shrieks of laughter from somewhere down the hall.

Rachel gave me a quick squeeze hello. "Shannon re-discovered my crimper."

Ah, yes. It was always fun to break into Rachel's many hair appliances. Looks like they'd started without me tonight.

Rachel grinned and tilted her head toward the kitchen. "And dinner's almost ready."

If we were having cinnamon rolls for dinner, it meant Rachel's health nut parents weren't home.

I set my overnight bag on the living room floor. "We've got the place to ourselves, then?"

"Yup, my parents said something about going out to a nice, quiet dinner where the oxygen isn't all being used up by giddy teenagers. Their words, not mine."

"Ha!" I sat down and scoured every surface for candy. "That's rich. Your mom is usually with us right up until she can't bear to watch us eat any more sugar."

Katie arrived next, looking exasperated. "I told my mom I was coming over here tonight, but she claimed I never told her, and it turned into this whole big thing where she didn't want to miss her shows by giving me a ride, and—" She shook her head and began to look around for sugar to consume. We're all a bit pathetic that way. Spotting me on the couch, Katie looked only momentarily surprised. "Annie! I feel like I haven't seen you around much outside of school." She sat down next to me and crushed me in a bear hug. Katie is the pitcher for our school's softball team and is even stronger than she looks.

"Here, take this and let me keep my lungs intact," I joked, handing her a bowl of jelly beans.

She gasped, scandalized. "Oooh, you were going to hide these from me, weren't you?!"

"Yup," I said. "And if you keep it quiet, I'll show you where Rachel hid the leftover Halloween candy."

A voice giggled from the hallway. "What are you two whispering about in here?"

I looked up to find that Shannon had outdone herself with the crimper. By the looks of things, she had also gotten into Rachel's collection of blue and pink hair spray. Katie let out a whoop of laughter, leaning on me for support and spilling the entire contents of the jelly bean bowl onto the floor.

I gave Shannon two thumbs up. "You look like punk rocker Barbie. Very nice."

Rachel walked in from the kitchen, already rolling her eyes. "Don't encourage her."

Liz was last to arrive, but she brought these delicious layered caramel apples with her—her specialty—and was forgiven. After getting settled, the first thing Liz did was give me a slight shoulder squeeze and a sad smile. "I'm glad you came. How is your family doing lately?"

I automatically launched into my speech about Daniel's progress, and Liz let me go on for a few minutes before gently prompting me. "What about everyone else?"

I froze, realizing I hadn't said a word about anyone but Daniel. It was just so much easier to tell people about him instead. "Well, honestly, things are so different now," I began slowly. "It's been weird. I was so excited for my mom and brother to come home and for things to get back to how they were, but it's not like that at all." My voice wavered but I kept going anyway. "My mom is always stressed out about appointments and bills and getting Daniel to do all his exercises at home, and it feels like she's a million miles away."

It was hard to keep the tears from falling, and before I knew it Liz was holding my hand and all eyes in the room were on me. Away from the lunch table at school, it felt only a little weird to open up to all of them like this. "I'm sorry. I don't mean to be such a downer."

Rachel placed a steaming mug of sweet-smelling tea in my trembling hands.

Shannon sunk down into a chair, sympathy all over her punk rocker Barbie face. "It's fine. You're allowed to have feelings, you know."

Katie awkwardly tossed a Kleenex box my way—it sailed too far to the right and hit the wall, knocking a family picture crooked before cartwheeling down to the floor. This broke the heavy mood and everyone cracked up. Katie isn't great with emotional stuff like this, but she tries.

"I feel better when I'm with you all, or anywhere I

know I can be myself and be free," I confessed. "I feel most like myself when I'm away from my family. Is that bad?"

Sympathetic looks all around, then Liz spoke into the silence. "This has been a crazy ordeal for your family and everything, and I know it can't be easy. But you do seem a little sad these days."

I blinked back tears and looked at the floor. If she thought *this* Annie was sad, I didn't want to think about what it would be like if I'd never met the Walkers. Probably I'd be a drooling puddle in some home for runaways if not for them, instead of just a semi-functional sad person. Thinking about the Walkers made me smile. "Well, I guess things aren't all bad."

Shannon ran up to me, wide-eyed, her colorful hair bouncing. "I knew it. Annie has boy-crazy all over her face."

"*What?*" roared Rachel, scandalized. "Annie, have you been holding out on me?"

I couldn't control the giggles, and a hot blush crept across my cheeks. "Well, I guess there *is* someone."

Rachel raised one eyebrow. "Who?"

"Owen." His face flashed in my mind as I said his name. "His sister Jenna is a patient at the hospital. We're… I've gotten pretty close to their family, being at the hospital so much. And their mom is so easy to talk to. It's great having people around who understand me when it feels like my family doesn't."

I could tell Rachel was trying hard to look supportive

and not say something like *"But I understand you, and I took care of you the best I could."* Maybe she knew it meant something different to have people around you who were going through the same things you were.

Liz cut in. "Oh you *totally* have a crush on him. Does this mean you're over that guy from your church?"

"You mean Travis?" I was shocked to realize I hadn't been thinking about him in that way at all lately. The total giddiness he used to conjure was altogether like something from a different life. When had *that* happened? Maybe I was beginning to see he was a better friend than I'd judged him to be, and that meant more to me than some silly crush.

I straightened up and smiled at her. "Yes, I believe I am."

Rachel still looked suspicious. "I'll alert the media. But in the meantime, when do we get to meet this *Owen* of yours?"

Liz jumped up, clapping her hands together. "I know! Annie, you should ask him to the dance!"

"What dance?"

"You know, the one they always do before Christmas," Rachel said dismissively, clearly agitated I was missing the point. "That's a great idea, Liz!"

Liz nodded enthusiastically.

Me, ask Owen to the dance? I guess I could. Would he say yes? Would it be weird? What would he think of my friends? And most importantly, how cute would he look all dressed up?

Liz broke through my daydream. "Your FACE, Annie!" She and Shannon laughed.

I rolled my eyes and sighed theatrically. "Fine, I will make this huge sacrifice and ask the guy I like to the dance."

"You'd better!" said Rachel. "I need to approve this person immediately, or I'm cutting you off from any and all sugar for the rest of your life."

The rest of the evening was marvelous. I felt a rush of nerves and excitement when I thought of Owen, and dreamt of us arriving at the dance together, arm in arm, beaming and beautiful and walking ten feet off the ground.

Chapter 23

I didn't have to sit with my nerves for long. The very next day it was time for another Walker visit. Mom, Daniel, and I passed through the thick metal doors to the hospital's main lobby, Mom and I walking slowly so Daniel and his brace-clad leg could keep up, my mind alive and buzzing about the whole Owen situation. When we got to the elevators I hung back. I wanted to be alone with my thoughts.

"Six-thirty," Mom said over her shoulder, as she took Daniel's right hand and led him into the elevator. Mom pressed a button, and before the door closed I could see her face had already transformed into what I liked to call *therapy mode*. Therapy mode was when she looked at you but didn't see you, because already she was running through the multitude of questions she always brought to Daniel's physical therapists. Also, it meant that inside she was steeling herself for the emotional onslaught that was Daniel's therapy. She'd sit helplessly while someone else manipulated Daniel's previously perfect little-boy limbs. She'd gulp back the guilt she felt because Daniel could no longer play Little League baseball. She'd paste on a firm, brave face while she took thorough notes on Daniel's progress, the therapist's instructions for next time, and anything else she thought might help.

I knew this. I saw it when I came back from visiting the Walkers once, and Daniel's therapy was just finishing up. And I saw the tears falling on her impeccable notes when she thought nobody was looking.

I was still thinking about therapy mode when I stepped out of the elevator onto Jenna's floor. But my thoughts turned to Owen as I rounded the corner into Jenna's room. There was no way Owen could say no, right? After all, I'd just picked up a secret weapon from Nora.

"So, what's his name?" Jenna's colorless face rested on her pillow but her eyes sparked with mischief.

"I'll bet I know," Nancy said, which set her and Jenna into giggles.

My face burned hot, and I jumped about a mile when I noticed Owen behind me in the doorway. His fair skin was red to the tips of his ears as he mumbled something about "Wannatakeawalkwithme?"

My heart pounded as I hid a smile and stuck out my tongue at the giggles behind us. "Sure."

When we were safely down the hall, I reached into my back pocket and pulled out my secret weapon. "I have something for you." I held out five Band-Aids.

Owen's eyes widened with immediate recognition. "This one's a super rare glow-in-the-dark Harry Potter! And SpongeBob SquarePants! Where'd you get these?"

"Not telling. But these are actually bribes, if you can believe it."

"What for?" Owen inspected the other Band-Aids as best he could through their wrappers.

I found a freckle on his forehead to focus on. "Well, there's this dance at my school. It's next weekend and it's being held in our crappy gym and I was wondering if you'd maybe want to go. Uh, with me." I risked a look slightly south of the freckle.

Owen was smiling. "Sure, I'll go." He looked at the Band-Aids again and his smile widened. "Thanks for these. I actually have something for you, too. Close your eyes and hold out your hand."

I felt his fingers brush mine as he placed something small and light into my outstretched palm.

"Ok, open."

I looked down to find in my humble hand the crown jewel of all pens. Nora's pen. There were no words. This felt like the nicest thing anyone had done for me in a long time, and it was just a pen. But not just a pen.

I smiled up at Owen in awe and wonder. "It's the most magnificent gift in the entire world. Thank you."

There was a "hee-hee" from behind Owen, and I caught the last glimpse of Nora's scrubs as she rounded the corner and scurried back down the corridor.

I had a date to the dance, and I had a fabulous pen. Best day ever!

Owen and I strolled back into Jenna's room, serenaded by more giggles from Jenna and Nancy. I tried to focus on not smiling on the outside as big as I was smiling on the inside. A girl has to keep *some* secrets, you know.

Owen and I had an understanding after that. I didn't think of it as a boyfriend/girlfriend thing, we just liked being around each other and didn't need to define anything beyond that.

Nobody else understood. Least of all Rachel. When I caught up with her at church on Sunday I blurted out the good news about Owen and the dance, only to discover that I couldn't describe the other events in a way that made any sense to her.

"So you gave him some Band-Aids, and he gave you a pen? Romantic. An exchange of medical supplies and office wares. I believe you two might be considered nerdy man and wife in some cultures. But did he kiss you? Did he ask you out or anything after he gave you your…pen?"

I smiled. "Not exactly."

It was all impossible to describe, and part of me liked that. It was as if trying to put words to what happened— assign regular, everyday words to pinpoint how I felt— would take away some of the magic.

It was necessary to let Tracy in on things, too. I had

run to her in a blind panic after returning from the hospital that night. I was so focused on asking Owen, I hadn't realized I didn't even have anything to wear to the dance. I knocked on her door and entered when I heard an uncharacteristically subdued "Come in."

Tracy looked tired, but her face brightened a little when I bounded into her room, plopped down beside where she was sitting cross-legged on her bed with phone in hand, and said dramatically, "I need expert help."

She cocked one eyebrow. "Clearly. What's up?"

"I don't have anything to wear to the dance. The dance I'm going to with...Owen."

Tracy set down her phone, crossed her arms, and tried her best to look disapprovingly at me. "Who's Owen? Why have I never heard about him?"

I could feel myself blushing. "Trace...before now there was nothing to tell. He was just Owen, but now he's *Owen*."

She nodded knowingly.

I decided to change the subject before she got any other details out of me. "I was going to ask Mom to take me somewhere to look at dresses, but...I can't ask her that."

"You can't ask Mom," she echoed, her eyes clouding over briefly. It struck me how Tracy must have felt like I felt—that our mom was now a million miles away, living her days and nights in a place where girls needing dresses for dances was just not important. I made a mental note to ask Tracy about her own struggles later. I wasn't brave enough to do it now.

We hung out until bedtime, her talking about her various love interests and me finally spilling the details about Owen. She listened thoughtfully and watched my face closely as I told her how seen and special he made me feel. I even showed her the pen.

She inspected it, clicking the purple plastic brain a few times for good measure. "This is all it took to win you over? A used pen?"

I shrugged. "It lights up."

Tracy laughed and tossed the pen into my outstretched hands. "Of course it does." She shook her head and smiled. "In that case, I think I have something that'll work."

She strolled to her closet, starting to thumb through the dresses at the far end. I held my breath and tried to peek around her. Wearing one of Tracy's dresses?! This was more than I dared to hope for. I thought she'd offer to drive me somewhere and help me pick out a dress, since under normal circumstances she doesn't let me anywhere near her closet under penalty of banishment.

She turned around and held out a dress with a black velvet top and shimmering gold skirt. I smiled, feeling my eyebrows rise.

She tossed it my way before resuming her search. "Try that one…might fit."

She didn't need to tell me twice. I scrambled off her bed and changed into the dress before she could change her mind. Then I sighed and scrutinized my appearance in her full-length mirror. It didn't look quite right, not even when I twirled the skirt.

Tracy turned to study me. "So that's a no." She instead tossed me a floor-length burgundy spaghetti-strapped dress. "This one instead. You look ridiculous in that."

"Rude!" I laughed, but changed into it anyway. The soft fabric hugged my skin as I slipped it on, and I was shocked to see that the dress fit perfectly.

"That's the one," Tracy agreed, nodding as I did a 360. "We'll curl your hair, and I'll do your makeup. Crisis averted."

I beamed at her, grateful once again to have a big sister to save the day. I wondered if I'd ever be able to return the favor. For now, we were two happy sisters and it felt just like old times.

Chapter 24

Owen arrived at my house right on time the night of the dance. When I opened the door, he blushed a little and shoved a clear plastic box into my hands. He brought me a corsage, and I didn't even get him anything.

"My mom picked it out and forced me to bring it," Owen explained.

I laughed and stepped back to take in the sight of him. He looked nice all dressed up. He was wearing khakis and a dark blue button-down shirt. It also looked like he had spent some time trying to tame his wild hair, but to no avail. There were still a couple of random red corkscrews that refused to sit nicely, and I found that oddly comforting.

I gave him a quick hug. "You look like such a stud, Owen!"

Owen made an *Awww, shucks* face, his eyes soft. "Yeah, right. But you! You look really pretty."

Courtesy of Tracy I was all dressed up and styled, barely resembling the everyday Annie he knew. Like my very own fairy godmother, Tracy had turned me into a Cinderella before vanishing in a cloud of fairy dust with plans of her own. "Thanks." I smiled at Owen and stepped aside to let him in the house.

His expression changed as he tilted his head and looked past me. I followed his gaze and noticed he was looking at one of the eye charts Daniel used for therapy. I smiled awkwardly at Owen. He understood about having a sibling in the hospital, but how much would he understand about how afterwards, with some kids like Daniel, there's so much lost and so much work to be done to get it back?

As if on cue, Daniel appeared from the hallway. "Who are you?" he asked unceremoniously, eyeing Owen with mingled interest and suspicion.

"I'm taking your sister to the dance, my name's—"

"Wanna see my new bike?" Daniel interrupted.

Owen's face registered shock, then neutralized. Was he expecting the guard dog routine from my scrawny little brother? Please.

"Sure." Owen followed Daniel down the hall with a helpless shrug my way. Poor Owen, I probably could've warned him about that. Daniel's new bike was something no visitor to the Spencer home had the luxury of avoiding these days. My parents had found a mountain bike that could be modified with special pedals and handlebars so Daniel could secure his weak left hand and foot.

Meanwhile, there I stood. This was not off to a great start. Is this how it was supposed to go? *Annie's Expert Book of Dating, Chapter 1: What to do when your date arrives to pick you up, becomes distracted by your little brother's new bike, and you are left standing there alone with his mom honking the horn in the driveway.* How romantic.

I sighed and glared at Daniel's eye chart on the wall. Come to think of it, our house probably looked pretty weird to Owen. There was therapy stuff absolutely everywhere. I knew as Daniel led Owen down the hall, he would have to sidestep an exercise ball or two and likely wouldn't miss the piles of MRI films on the counter. And that was just the stuff you could see without looking for it. I knew most cupboards now held a small hand exerciser for building strength, just like I knew the piles on the table held insurance papers and therapy schedules. *Daniel took over everything*, I thought with a flash of bitterness as I spotted his folded-up walking cane lying on the ground.

I bent down to pick it up, determined to at least hide what I could of Daniel's stuff. Even if Owen understood, I wanted this night to be about anything but Daniel. Then again, I realized with some dismay that the physical therapy equipment around the house was probably less noticeable to Owen than the spectacle that was Daniel himself. He still wore his arm and leg braces most of the time because they kept his tendons stretched out so everything could loosen up and heal properly from his stroke. He was also still adapting to his slackened facial muscles, and it was sometimes downright impossible to understand what he was saying.

A noise from the dining room caught my attention and I realized Mom was in there. These days the hospital bills and insurance claim papers just kept coming. Every day at least half of the mail we got went straight to Mom's command center to sort, and there was so much stuff to organize that it spilled over onto the dining room table now, too.

She was talking on the phone. As I watched, she hung up and began crying into her hands. My breath caught in my throat, and a wave of helplessness washed over me. She couldn't catch a break. My heart started pounding when I heard Daniel's voice growing louder as he and Owen made their way back out to where I stood, frozen in place.

Without warning, the front door opened and Nancy waltzed in. "Shake a leg, lovebirds!"

Daniel gaped at her, and Owen looked indignant. "Mom, what line of reasoning did you use to barge into someone else's house without knocking?"

"It's 'cuz my kids are in here," she said, smiling at me and turning to extend her hand to Daniel. "How do you do, sir? I'm Owen's chauffeur for the evening." She was using an outrageously cringe-worthy British accent, and Daniel giggled.

I laughed too, noticing there were no more sounds of crying coming from the dining room. I turned to see my mom coming toward us.

"Well, take it easy, man," Nancy said to Daniel, going on to engage in an elaborate secret handshake with my brother, arm brace and all.

Mom's voice, sounding formal, floated over my head. "You must be Nancy."

Nancy straightened. "That's me! And you must be Annie's mother. How lovely to finally meet you. We've all been so spoiled to get to spend so much time with your wonderful daughter."

"Yes, she sure does seem to love spending time with your family." Mom sounded a little too crisp and controlled, even though the words were all polite.

Owen looked at me, one eyebrow up.

If Nancy noticed, she did a great job of pretending otherwise. "This is my son, Owen." She smiled at him and tried to flatten a wayward curl. "We promise he does not have a criminal record."

Mom paused for a beat and then simply said, "Nice to meet you both. Have a nice time," already turning to resume her post. As we walked down the driveway, I tried to chase away the vision stuck in my head: Mom standing behind me, a little too straight and still. But there was something else. Mom crying alone at the table, Mom wrestling day and night trying to make people on the other end of that phone care about Daniel's situation,

Mom crushed under the weight of so many problems she couldn't solve. But what could I do to help? What could any of us do?

As soon as we were outside, Nancy beamed at me with extra glitter in her eyes. "Annie, you look simply breathtaking." Her eyes came to rest on the corsage I held. "Owen! You're supposed to put that corsage *on* her."

Owen looked pained as Nancy took the box from me, opened it, and slid the elastic band over my wrist. It was a beautiful arrangement, three small white roses and some glittery blue ribbon intertwining them.

My first corsage, and it was absolutely perfect. "Thank you. It's really lovely."

She smiled. "We've got a lot of rough edges to wear down on this young man here, but someday he'll learn how to treat a lady."

I laughed as Owen pantomimed creating a noose and putting his neck into it. We got to the school and stepped out of the car, Nancy honking as she exited the parking lot.

Owen rolled his eyes. "My mom. Subtle as always. Hey—back at your house, were our moms about to fight over you?"

I laughed and shook my head in disbelief. "Yeah. There was a little something weird there, right? What was that about? Maybe I was supposed to introduce them before now, or something?"

"Who knows. But most importantly, who would win

in a cage match? My mom's actually pretty scrappy, but your mom has righteous indignation on her side."

"Maybe costumes would help." Our laughter echoed off the pavement and disappeared into the night.

Owen's face turned suddenly thoughtful. "You know, my mom does think of you as one of her own. I think she sees me, and she sees you, and we're like two chances to do the same thing right. She's trying to save you like she's trying to save me."

Owen tucked a loose curl behind my ear. My skin tingled where he touched it.

When we got inside the gym I spotted Rachel right away. She was already on the dance floor with some guy I'd seen once or twice around school—Rachel is sweet and stunning and never has trouble finding anyone to dance with. She would probably be out there all night if she found someone who could keep up with her.

Rachel was for sure sizing Owen up from afar, and Owen—bless him—pretended not to notice as she gave me two enthusiastic thumbs up.

Movement on the other side of the gym caught my eye as I saw Katie, waving to me and beaming at the comically tall guy she was standing next to. I recognized him from the basketball team.

Owen and I had a great night. I dutifully introduced him to Rachel as she bounced and swayed under the strobe lights and pounding music. We found Liz and Shannon before catching up with Katie and her date—I named him

Gigantor in my head—laughing together as we saw Rachel had already worn out two dance partners and was busy searching for her next victim.

I felt a little guilty for being out having so much fun, though. In all honesty there was probably something I could've done to help my mom, but instead I was here. Daughter of the year award, here I come.

Owen spoke softly, breaking into my thoughts. "Want to go outside for a second?"

We excused ourselves from Katie and Gigantor, me dodging the knowing wink she shot my way. Owen followed as I snuck through the side door leading to an outdoor basketball court. As the door closed behind us I breathed a sigh of relief at how quiet it instantly became. I guess I had just gotten used to the noise.

I smiled down at my corsage, happy to have a keepsake from this magical night. "I'm glad you came."

Owen smiled and sat down on a nearby bench. "Me too. This has actually been pretty fun, and your friends are nice."

"Rachel was going to kill me if I didn't introduce you."

He laughed. "She's the one who goes to your church, right?"

"Yeah. She's been my best friend since we were little. But I also feel super close to Jenna. Rachel is like a steady, cheerful teal that is always looking out for you, and there's some glitter you can see when the light hits just right. And

Jenna…she's like…*magenta*. Fun, bright, impossible to ignore."

Owen smiled and nodded thoughtfully. It was the first time I'd ever told anybody out loud about the colors. He stared off into the darkness, and I wondered what he saw out there. When I looked at the world with Owen beside me, I saw how the hardship of family illness was like a new face you wore. Something that made you different from everyone else and changed the way you looked in a way that was only recognizable to people who understood. Or maybe it was like a dark mist had found its way into both of our lives, curling and settling around us—permanent, even though it was unwanted. And perhaps Owen and I recognized each other's dark mist and found comfort in the familiarity of it.

"Owen, can I ask you something?"

He turned to look at me, his green eyes warm. "Sure."

"Do you think you and I are damaged goods, and that's why we get along?"

He laughed. "Oh, for sure. I recognized your same deer-in-the-headlights look and it was an instant attraction."

"I think you're right. We both have the same rainy gray of *What in the world am I going to make myself for dinner tonight?*"

He rolled his eyes, and that made me smile. "What else? What's *my* color?"

I looked closer, noticing that while his eyes were the

same shape and color as Jenna's, they hid something I'd never seen in hers. I sat back. "Are you sure you want me to say?"

He nodded. "Out with it."

I scratched an itch on the back of my neck and avoided his eyes. "You have the forest green of peace and loyalty and some delightful quirkiness, but there's also something far too serious hiding in there. Something jet black."

Owen stared at me, eyes wide. "What does that mean?"

I shrugged. "You tell me."

Owen's shoulders drooped and he looked at the ground. There was silence, and then he gave up. "You might as well know."

Chapter 25

"It was the first time we'd been out on the boat all season," Owen began. "It was just me, my mom, and Jenna."

I nodded and tried to find clues from Owen's face about what was coming. He was impossible to read, and his voice became different as he spoke. Slower. Tortured. "Jenna wanted to water ski, and my mom said she was too worn out to steer the boat but I could do it if I promised to be careful."

I pretended not to notice as a tear skimmed Owen's face and he hurriedly brushed it away.

"There was another boat." His voice rose as the tears came faster. "It was ahead of us and I must've turned too late to miss it. And my mom looked away just for a second because her hat blew off, and I heard yelling...and I looked back...and Jenna hadn't seen the other boat. She hit it full force, and I panicked. I couldn't see her, and Mom was screaming 'What happened?!' And a guy on the other boat was shouting that she hadn't let go of the cord and she'd gone under, and he dove off the boat to find her."

I gulped and closed my eyes, willing myself not to picture the scene.

"They brought her up and there was blood everywhere, and she wasn't breathing. She had to be airlifted out. They put her on a board and she was like a rag doll—her legs and her arm, it didn't look right." Owen put his head in his hands. "She was under their boat all broken, just trying to reach the surface…and she found their propeller instead. They turned it off but not fast enough. Every single night I have nightmares about it. Seeing it happen over, and over, and over."

I placed a hand lightly on Owen's quivering shoulder, and as he turned toward me I held him tight without hesitation.

"It's my fault!" he wailed.

"No."

"But look what happened to her because of me. I did this to her!"

"NO," I said again, louder. "It was a terrible accident, but it was still an accident. You didn't mean to do it."

And his tears were my tears, and I tried to understand and maybe I could, a little. We sat without speaking and he knew I wasn't going anywhere. It was all I had to give, but I knew it was what he needed most.

When Mom picked me up from the dance that night, I felt like a completely different person. I'd been sitting there with Owen, holding his hand, waiting for our moms and thinking about Jenna and how long she'd been in the hospital. Had I ever thought to ask how long she'd been there before I met her? Considering what happened to her I guess a long hospital stay wasn't all that surprising, but it still seemed like something else must be wrong. I vowed to ask her directly when I saw her next. No letting her gloss over the truth or believing her when she said the pain wasn't all that bad. Mom pulled out of the parking lot and was driving a little bit faster than usual.

"Do you know what happened last week at the hospital after our therapy visit?"

Her tone was sharp, and I could tell I was not supposed to answer this question. "I was waiting for you by Nora's station, and I heard her telling some nurses all about her little match-making scheme with you and that boy. And I had to stand there and pretend like I knew what they were talking about, so they wouldn't look at me like I was the most negligent mother in the world because I didn't know all the details of your love life. You seem perfectly happy to have found yourself a new family, all while I'm trying to hold *this* family together."

I was speechless, but a flame of indignation burned hot in my chest.

She kept going. "So why is that? Huh? Why does my

own child prefer to be with strangers when her own family is just trying to heal and make it through?"

That did it. I was shaking with rage. "They aren't strangers. I was lucky to find people in that hospital who cared about how I was doing and who I didn't have to walk on eggshells around. You guys never paid attention to me, so I found people who did. What's wrong with that?"

I was crying now, and I knew it wasn't a fair fight. But I didn't care. It was now or never to get all this stuff out into the open. I was so tired of being patient, of trying to understand things that were just plain unfair. "Mom, don't you think I'd rather feel like I belong with my own family? Don't you think that given the choice, I would've been taking walks with you? Having ice cream with you? Talking to you about what was going on in my life? Well, I tried that and I got nowhere. I *still* get nowhere because you're too wrapped up with Daniel. So why should I keep trying?"

We were in the driveway now, and Mom stared straight ahead as she jammed the car out of gear and snapped off the headlights. "How about you? A daughter so selfish she doesn't think to acknowledge the things her mother does for her. The night of your dance recital I left Daniel's side knowing full well he was about to suffer even more. I left him and came to see you dance because it was important to you. How can you sit there and say you're so neglected?"

I was stunned. So she had seen me, after all? "I didn't know that. How could I have known? You were already in the car, you didn't say a word about it, and you launched right into the bad news about Daniel."

"I tried as best I could to be there for you," she shot back angrily. "I'm sorry if that's not good enough."

Mom unbuckled her seatbelt, grabbed her purse, and was out of the car before I could respond.

Chapter 26

I t was Christmas Eve day, and the house was silent. A light, freezing drizzle fell from the sky, but inside it didn't feel cozy. Christmas at the Spencer home was usually packed with fun traditions, but this year things felt different. The stockings were hanging above the fireplace, but there were no lights or candles adorning the green garland placed askew on the mantle. No colorful Christmas lights graced the insides of bedroom windows. Plus, Christmas usually meant tons of baking. There were the special apple pies we made from scratch only once a year. And then the spice bread we'd drizzle with icing. There were sugar cookies with homemade frosting and sprinkles, and I always got to be the one to roll out the cookie dough and press in the angel and Christmas tree cookie cutters, because Mom said I was so careful and never rolled out the dough too thick or too thin.

I always looked forward to it, but it seemed like Mom forgot all about it this year. Ever since our fight in the car after the dance, things had been icy and tense between us. I guess we were each trying to hold out longer to prove we were right, but that felt less and less important as the days dragged on. I missed the heavenly smells of our Christmas baking, almost as much as I missed being the quiet kid nobody worried about.

I sat on the couch with my journal and tried not to think about how much had changed since last year. I gazed at the Christmas tree on the other side of the living room. It's tradition for us to all gather around it every year and put the ornaments on, laughing and remembering which ornament we'd each gotten in years past. I saw the ornament boxes had been dragged to where the Christmas tree was, but there were none on the tree. I crept across the room and opened one of the boxes. Years of happy family memories and celebrated milestones winked out at me, and I lovingly lifted the first few ornaments out of the box. What would we get to remember this year's events? Did they make an ornament for *My first brain tumor* or maybe *A million tears shed in public places*?

Dad was at the church, Tracy was out with some friends, and Mom had taken Daniel to his monthly checkup with Dr. Gill. Normally I'd tag along to see Jenna, but they had left before I was awake. If we were going to have ornaments, it was going to have to be me.

Pretty soon Tracy flew in, then came Mom and Daniel, and for a while the house was alive with activity as we all got ready to go to the candlelight service we always have at church on Christmas Eve.

Merry Christmas from Aspen! came a text from Rachel as we rode to church. *So sorry I won't be at the service tonight.*

A picture popped through of Rachel making a face while holding a forkful of a mushy-looking brown substance.

I laughed to myself. *Please tell me that's not...*

Yes, Ma'am! Nothing says Merry Christmas like a nice, dry tofurkey.

We got to church and settled in, with Daniel sitting next to Mom as usual. It didn't bother me anymore. Nothing dark could touch me right now. This was my favorite service of the year, so reverently warm and beautifully still. Every year Tracy sings a solo during the time when everyone's candles are lit, and this year she chose "O Holy Night." I watched the ripple of candlelight spread as Tracy's voice floated delicately overhead. A palpable hum of peace held us all as she finished singing and Dad said a prayer.

After the service, lots of people hung around to wish each other Merry Christmas. I noticed it didn't feel like I was being singled out or watched, instead I melted into the glowing atmosphere like everybody else.

I spotted Travis and he gave me a small wave as he walked over.

"Merry Christmas," he said.

"Merry Christmas to you, too."

"How have things been going lately?"

I shrugged. "It's still an adjustment having everyone under one roof, but I'm trying to remember what you said. Daniel's got it tough and there are people out there who know I'm going through things, too."

Travis nodded. "Good. It'll take time, but things will get better. Maybe not back to how they used to be, but that's life, right?"

I smiled, wondering where on earth Travis got all this deep life wisdom. I caught a glimpse of my mom just over his shoulder, and my smile faltered. Would things get better? Or was everything so messed up for my family that not even Christmas could fix it? "I guess."

It was late by the time we all got home. Usually on Christmas Eve we made a fire in the fireplace and gathered around Dad as he read us the Christmas story from the Bible. It was always so warm and lovely; we'd snack on the goodies Mom and I made, and Mom and Dad would say something nice about each of us kids. Maybe something they appreciated about us, or ways they'd seen us grow during the past year. After that we would open our stockings, and sometimes we could convince Mom and Dad to let us each choose a gift from under the tree to open. Later we'd all drift off to bed, feeling warm and loved and happy.

Tonight, though, we were all too tired to think about anything but bed. It probably would've taken a miracle to rally everyone and continue with the traditions. It felt sad and a little empty to turn out the lights on Christmas Eve and just go to sleep, wondering what Jenna, Owen, and Nancy were doing that night. I wanted to be with them so badly and the tears came without warning. I could see the smile that would light up Jenna's face, the way Owen would laugh and blush, the way Nancy would wrap me in a hug the next time I saw them all. I wished it could be now. Especially because I had a renewed, gnawing worry about Jenna. She was going to get better, right? How long would that take?

Even though it was late, I grabbed my phone to send her a text. *Not to spoil the surprise, but I got you some skates for Christmas. You, me, roller derby. You in?*

When I groggily opened my eyes Christmas morning, I saw I had a reply from Jenna. *I love you. I'll be there. Merry Christmas!*

I shuffled into the living room to find Daniel already there, gazing up at the un-lit Christmas tree. "How long have you been up?"

"Feels like hours." He pointed to the tree. "Something's missing and I couldn't figure out what it was. But I just realized there are no candy canes."

I looked—he was right. I chuckled to myself. *Really, kid? Of all the things that are different this year, it's the candy canes for you??* Oh well, I did what I could. I plugged the lights in and the tree blazed to life, colorful lights dancing in the chill of the early morning. Daniel smiled his lopsided smile, and I sat down next to him, and we waited for the others to come.

"Merry Christmas, Annie."

"Merry Christmas, Daniel."

Chapter 27

When I finally got the chance to visit Jenna, I was bursting at the seams. I was worried and had so many questions for her about the accident—stuff I couldn't exactly send in a text. There was so much to talk about…it was a serious long shot, but I hoped Owen hadn't already told her the story of how our moms had a mild standoff in my living room. Also, would she be willing to engage in girl talk with me about her own brother? She'd already asked how the dance went and I had left out any mushy details, only telling her we had a great time. On the drive over I quietly organized my thoughts, fearing that as soon as I opened my mouth everything would come tumbling out in one huge mess.

When we got to the hospital Mom said a curt "Six-thirty" reminder as we parted ways at the elevators. Would things ever be normal between us? And what was "normal" now, anyway? Was this version of my mom the best I could hope for? Every time I felt bad enough to own up to my share of the blame and smooth things over, I remembered all over again that I was the kid and she was the parent. Wasn't it her job to patch things up and apologize for pushing me away? There were some hurts that ran too deep to be glossed over and forgotten.

I was so lost in thought I nearly passed right by Jenna's room.

Rolling my eyes at my carelessness, I turned the knob and was about to push it when my eyes caught sight of something strange. Instead of the thin black spiky writing declaring Jenna Walker the occupant of this room, there was a new name scrawled in.

The corridor suddenly felt far too small, with walls that tilted and swayed. I blinked my eyes once. Twice. Focused with all my might on the name that wasn't Jenna's.

A coherent thought broke through. *Of course!* I scolded myself for becoming so panicked over nothing. They must've moved her again.

"Hi there, Annie."

I spun around to find Dr. Gill standing there.

"I saw your mom and Daniel just now, and thought you'd be here too." The look on his face was one I'd seen before, when he had bad news.

"Where's Jenna?" I asked, trying to keep my tone casual.

He ignored my question. "So Nora tells me you are something of a pen collector, is that true?"

Oh great, what was this about? Was I four years old

and he was going to pat me on the head and give me a balloon? Dr. Gill reached into his jacket. He pulled out a plain Bic rollerball stick pen and handed it to me.

"Uh, wow." It didn't even have a lid. "Thanks, Dr. Gill."

He looked quite pleased with himself, and I could see the mental scorecard adding another tally mark in the *good bedside manner with patients' families* column.

"I need to find Jenna," I said. It was not a question this time.

Dr. Gill sighed and lowered his voice. "Annie, I'm sorry to be the one to tell you this, but—"

Nancy rounded the corner. When she saw me her tight expression broke apart, and she sped toward me. "Oh, Annie," Nancy sobbed as she crashed into me and held me tight. "She's gone."

Dr. Gill's disembodied voice came from somewhere behind us. "I'm so sorry."

There had to be some mistake. I could feel my throat struggling for air as if all of it had been forcibly removed from the building. *No. It isn't true!* I broke free from Nancy and ran from the hallway, ran from Jenna's room. My heart pounded and my brain spat out fragments of confusion and shock. I should have realized sooner that something was seriously wrong. Why hadn't I paid more attention? The tears could only be kept at bay for so long as the shock gave way to the reality forcing its way in. I nearly ran over two doctors and a nurse in my frantic attempt to get outside. I finally reached the front doors of the hospital and burst forth into cool late-afternoon air, the tears coming faster now, my aching throat protesting painfully. *Not here...not here...*

I ran until I came upon a bench by the lake, and my body released wracking, uncontrollable sobs. The tears came from everywhere in my body, from deep inside as the heartbreak refreshed itself with each ragged breath I took. The tears came for Jenna first. That much didn't take any effort at all; it was right there at the surface. For now I could only think about her as an idea, and not think of the specifics. Not her ringing laugh or how she was part hummingbird, Jenna who was certainly too young to die. It made me want to be numb, to disappear into the cool, dark water where I didn't have to think about the brilliant magenta of Jenna's smile fading...fading...away.

Tears came for Daniel too, for the guilt of knowing everything he'd lost, and for pitying him, and for wishing none of this had ever happened. I cried for my family, for sleepless nights and unanswered questions and *Why, God?* I cried for me.

The winter sun was melting, reflecting onto the lake as I sat there trying to make sense of the fact that Jenna was gone, wishing with all my heart that I could talk to her one last time.

Nancy's shaky voice materialized beside me. "You mind walking an old woman around for old time's sake?" As much as it hurt, I owed her at least this much.

"I'm so sorry I just ran off," I managed to choke out.

Nancy waved away the words. "It's really okay."

We made our way slowly around the lake where we'd walked together so many times before. I spoke numbly into the heavy silence. "What happened to her?"

Fresh tears spilled onto Nancy's face. "It happened so fast. The doctors said there was a lot of internal damage to her kidneys that they didn't see because of how bad her other injuries were. She fought so hard and she never let on how much pain she was in, but ultimately it was just too much. Even for her. Owen and I came to see her today and she started to say her goodbyes. She spoke with Owen alone, and when I came back in, she said she loved us, but she needed to go. And then she was gone, and they couldn't bring her back. Just like that—all that was left of our spitfire Jenna was this broken, worn-out body."

I couldn't picture this, it was too hard. "And Owen?"

Nancy shook her head. "You and Owen, cut from the same cloth. I figured I'd come down here and find where at least one of you ran off to."

In spite of everything, I managed a small laugh.

Nancy chuckled, too. "Do I have an offensive smell? How come you both thought it best to bolt from my presence?"

And then laughing turned to crying, and Owen was beside us, his eyes wide and incandescent with pain. The three of us stood there in the cold, each trapped in our own thoughts. My mind and heart were swirling with anguish and disbelief. How had I arrived at the hospital *just* a little too late to say goodbye? Had she been waiting for me? Holding on until she couldn't do it anymore? It was too painful to imagine, but knowing Jenna, I wouldn't be surprised.

Daniel's uncertain voice came from behind me. "Mom says it's time to go home, Annie."

Nancy gave me a hug and I made sure I wasn't the first one to let go. I knew she would cry long into the night. She and Owen, looking so small and so sad, would go home and force each other to eat something every once in a while. They'd laugh as they remembered things Jenna had said and done, and cry when the pain became too heavy. And that's really where I belonged.

Daniel led me back to the hospital parking lot. "Dr. Gill told us about your friend…I'm sorry." His little face was so earnest it made me cry all over again.

I placed my hand lightly on his head. "Thanks, Daniel."

I felt dazed all the way home. Everything I'd been saving inside to say to Jenna now hung in the air like an over-inflated balloon. Yet it was all so trivial compared to what I would've told her if I got to see her one last time. I would've thanked her for seeing who I truly was and celebrating that person, with no changes or hiding or apologies required. I would've told her she changed my life.

When we got home and approached the front door, I sensed Mom wanted to tell me something. I looked at her and she looked at me, and I could tell she knew this was not the time. I wasn't ready to talk about it, and she understood. And maybe that was a way to show care, too.

She reached out to touch my face, then opened the door and we walked in together. Her hand was on my shoulder, but not like when Nancy did it. My mom was tentative. I walked down the hall to my room, and she didn't follow.

I closed my bedroom door behind me, knowing there was only one place where I could be as sad as I wanted. I opened my closet door and stepped inside, careful to turn on the clip-on light before I closed the closet door. I sat down and hugged my knees to my chest, my eyes finding Owen's purple brain pen displayed in its prominent place on the bookshelf. I squeezed my eyes shut but it didn't stop the tears or the searing pain that ripped at my insides. Instead of feeling safe and hidden in my secret space, I felt suffocated. Like the closet was my coffin. And I had to get out.

Chapter 28

That whole first day after Jenna died, I didn't leave my room. Didn't leave my bed. I had visitors, but I couldn't remember much, and nobody stayed long.

I do remember Tracy kept coming in with trays of soup, crackers, juice, and things sick people eat, but I wasn't hungry. She sat on my bed and rubbed my back, and sang to me. Smokey situated himself at the foot of the bed and didn't leave once—not even when his little ears swiveled around to target the dry tinkling of his cat food being sprinkled into the bowl in the laundry room.

Rachel came in at one point, too. She'd brought me a small potted daisy and I could tell someone had told her the news and she'd racked her brain to think of something appropriate to do or say or give to me. And I knew she didn't fully understand what I had lost, but you've got to love a friend who will stick around through the awkward stuff with you and not just be there for the good times.

Because let's face it, the past few months had been pretty much *all* awkward stuff and very few good times.

The second day, I texted Nancy to check in on her. *How are you guys holding up?*

Oh, the usual, worst day ever. How are you? came her reply.

Same.

A long pause.

Funeral will be Saturday, noon. At the hospital, in the chapel on the third floor. Can you make it?

The thought of going to Jenna's funeral was such an absurd idea the very words shocked my system.

Of course. Wouldn't miss it.

Mom came into my room and drew back the curtains from my window. "You need to get out for a bit. Let's get you dressed, I've got something fun planned."

This was new. I numbly obeyed, curious about what kind of outing she had in mind. Hopefully it wasn't just one of Daniel's therapy sessions.

As it turned out, Mom had some Christmas returns to make at the mall. I think she knew I'd never turn down a trip—at least, the old me—and allowed me to come as a peace offering. Of course, Daniel was there too. Being with them in public was always an experience. Everywhere we went took twice as long because of Daniel's limp and Mom fussing over him.

We hadn't been there long when I heard it: the unmistakable sound of laughter at someone else's expense.

My head turned sharply in the direction of the sound, and I saw a group of boys standing across the corridor. Some of them I recognized from school, others looked older. As I stared at them, bewildered, it dawned on me who they were making fun of. One boy was modeling a stiff walk, dragging his left foot behind him while his left arm—fingers splayed unnaturally—flailed around. If I'm not mistaken, he was even drooling.

Something erupted inside me, and I felt instantly sick to my stomach. I stopped walking, clenching and unclenching my fists as my insides roared and I stared daggers at them. *How DARE they??*

They didn't understand what my family had been through. They had no idea of the pain, the tears. What made them think they had the right to stand there and make fun of him? I glanced at Daniel, praying he hadn't seen. He had. Mom, too. They both looked back at me, helpless and sad.

When Daniel's tormentors looked back his way, they saw me instead. I stood in front of Daniel and glared at them with all of the poison I could muster. I stared into each of their faces, daring them to continue.

They didn't. The rest of the time we spent there, I felt extremely aware of how people looked at Daniel. I noticed every stare, every double-take, every whispered comment from one person to another. And a rather obvious thought occurred to me: *He didn't ask for this to happen, and his life has changed forever.*

What Travis said about how Daniel had it tough, it made sense in a tangible way. I began to understand maybe a fraction of the protectiveness Mom felt—only, she had the whole world to protect Daniel from. His past to remember, his present to heal, his future to shape. All I had to do was be a big sister. And I could certainly do that.

Chapter 29

Saturday came all too fast. I asked Dad to come with me to the hospital for the funeral, and with sad eyes and a hand on my head, he agreed to.

I held his hand as we walked into the chapel on the third floor. I couldn't remember the last time I had done that, but it was nice having direct access to a minister at a time like this. As we signed the guest book and began to mix in with the other guests, Dad knew just how to act and exactly what to say. He'd been to his share of funerals, but this was my first one. It felt chaotic and desperately sad, like everyone in the room was looking around at everyone else, wondering who had the strongest claim to feeling the worst.

I spotted Nancy right away. I pointed her out to Dad, and he squeezed my hand as we made our way over. When she saw me, she stopped her conversation and wrapped me in a long hug. And Dad wasn't getting away. He got a big hug, too.

"Thank you both so much for coming. And I hope you're Annie's dad, otherwise I've created yet another awkward situation for myself."

Dad smiled and asked Nancy how she was feeling, in that great pastoral way he had. As the two of them talked, I chanced a peek around the room. The chapel was small, but maybe it was because there were so many people packed in. Patches of vibrant red hair wielded by people who were unmistakable blood relatives caught my eye. Everyone looked so stunned. I heard echoing snippets of "She was so young," "This is a tragedy," and "Poor Owen, losing his twin sister."

And where was Owen? I didn't see him anywhere. A crowd at my left shifted to reveal a glossy auburn coffin. My breath caught. The lid was up and a few of Jenna's untamable curls were all I could see, but that was too much. My hands went ice-cold. I had never seen a dead body before, and I certainly didn't want my first one to be Jenna. It felt backwards and wrong, like seeing her dead would erase all the life she brimmed with in my memory. What was I doing here? I couldn't stand in this suffocating chapel with Jenna lying there, dead, a few feet away.

Nobody noticed me slip out the chapel doors, and for once I was overjoyed to become invisible. I strode down the hallway toward the elevators, but turned and ran the other way when I heard Nora's voice floating toward me. I didn't have the strength to face even her right now.

I took the stairs down two at a time, my feet

automatically carrying me to the lake. I heard Owen before I saw him. The wailing of his broken heart sailed across the water and made me shiver. I found him sitting with his knees hugged up to his chest, his face hidden as he cried.

I sat down next to him.

If he was surprised, he didn't show it. He turned his watery eyes toward me, and I held his unwavering gaze. "I see it," he said. "The jet black...you have it too."

I looked away.

"You feel guilty because you think you should've been there when she died, and you feel like you should've asked her more how she was feeling. And you're angry you didn't get to say goodbye to her."

I nodded. "I feel like I failed her. And I feel completely disturbed at the thought of her up there in that box."

"I know. How can people hang out in there? Forget it—it's too morbid for me. I took one look at that coffin and bolted. Jenna would understand."

"Yes."

Owen picked at the dead remnants of what had in the springtime been a few blades of grass. "Before she died, Jenna asked to speak to me alone. She held my hand and said she knew I thought the accident was my fault, and she made me promise three times I wouldn't blame myself for it, because it was just an accident." Owen wiped his eyes and sniffed loudly. "Then she told me if I didn't take good care of you she'd haunt me and steal my Band-Aid collection."

I laughed a real laugh for the first time in what felt like forever. And then it was just us laughing, Owen and me, and it felt like we were regular kids hanging out by the lake on a Saturday.

"Look at you two, hiding down here when the party's upstairs."

My head snapped up and I was shocked to see Amanda standing on the sidewalk a few feet away. She didn't look as thin as she had the last time I saw her, and I could see some mature peach fuzz poking out from underneath the burgundy scarf she wore on her head.

Owen waved, and I stared at her, stunned.

"What—you didn't think I'd miss the big send-off for my dearly departed roommate, did you?"

I thought of how happy Jenna would be to know Amanda cared enough to pay her respects, and that made me smile.

"Too bad I couldn't stay in that teeny chapel for more than four seconds. Redheads creep me out. Seems unnatural."

Owen gazed at her, his face deadpan.

"No offense, of course," Amanda said breezily. As brave as Amanda was trying to be, I could see she'd been crying.

"So you hated seeing her in that coffin too, huh?" I asked Amanda.

"Absolutely, yes."

"It doesn't feel right," Owen said. "Funerals for people our age. I feel like there's got to be a better way, especially for Jenna."

Amanda smiled. "Wait here, I'll be right back."

Owen and I watched her scurry toward the hospital and go through the side entrance. After a few minutes she reappeared, walking slowly and balancing something she held to her chest with both arms.

"Ta-da!" She sat down next to us, handing a glass of water to first Owen, then me, keeping the last one for herself.

Before I could return Owen's shrug, Amanda pulled three packets of tea and fistfuls of something white from her pocket, dumping her treasure onto the ground in front of us.

Sugar packets.

Owen groaned. "Oh no."

"Yes!" Amanda laughed. "Don't you see? It's perfect!" She handed us each a packet of instant tea mix—plain, just like Jenna would've preferred.

I dumped the tea mix into my water, then picked up the closest sugar packet, tore the paper at the top, and watched the white crystals rush to dissolve in the brown tea water. "More appropriate than standing around, just staring at her body in a box and listening to everyone cry."

"Ugh." Owen picked up a few packets and got to work.

When the mound of sugar packets had been reduced to a massive wad of white paper, Amanda produced three plastic spoons and we stirred in solemn silence. "Now raise your glasses," she said, "To Jenna. Easily the most annoying roommate ever, who was simultaneously a huge pain in the butt, while also someone you'd miss if you were away from her for even five minutes."

"To Jenna," Owen and I chorused, as the three of us clinked glasses.

I watched Owen out of the corner of my eye as he scrunched up his face and brought his sugary tea closer. He closed his eyes and took a sip, gagging immediately.

He opened his eyes and caught Amanda and me laughing. "You guys didn't do it! How is that fair?"

"All right, all right," said Amanda. "To Jenna, who we will all see again soon after we consume what is most likely a lethal amount of sugar."

We clinked glasses, and this time we all drank.

"Fantastic," I lied.

Amanda shuddered. "Ready, get set, resting heart rate of one-hundred-eighty-seven!"

Owen raised his glass. "To Jenna. Whose death has left me traumatized for life, but at least I won't ever have to explain to one more person that yes, you can be twins even though one is a girl and one is a boy."

"To Jenna!" We clinked glasses, laughing, and took another drink.

"I'm beginning to see lots of rainbows," Owen said. "This explains so much about Jenna."

My turn. I cleared my throat and held up my glass. "To

Jenna, the rarest of creatures. A girl disguised as a paper doll, who was trying to turn herself into a hummingbird, probably to take her mind off the fact that Bob actually made her a Frankenstein."

"TO FRANKENSTEIN!" Owen and Amanda shouted together.

After the third drink, Amanda said she'd give Owen a dollar to chug the rest of his tea.

"Let me see the dollar first."

Amanda fished around in her pocket, revealing some string and a penny before triumphantly holding out a dollar bill for Owen's inspection.

"Okay, I'll do it." Closing his eyes, he tipped back his glass and chugged. But halfway through, he gagged and spat out the entire contents of his mouth.

"Gross!" Amanda yelled. "I definitely felt the spray from that."

"There were all these granules toward the bottom," Owen explained, wiping his mouth with the back of his hand. "I don't know how Jenna ever drank this. It's like five-hundred percent concentrated."

Suddenly a hand dove over my shoulder and grabbed my glass.

"To Jenna," said Nancy from behind us. "The daughter I repeatedly tried to pawn off, but really wouldn't have traded for the world." To my amazement, she downed the contents of my glass in a matter of seconds. When finished, she placed it upside-down on top of her head to prove it was empty.

"Smooth," she rasped as Amanda and I clapped.

I saw the glimmer of unshed tears in Nancy's eyes, but then they were gone and she was holding out her hand to collect Amanda's dollar.

"Gimmie."

Amanda handed over her dollar. "Nice work, Nancy."

"We're eatin' fancy tonight, boy!" Nancy said to Owen, who had buried his head in his hands.

"Out-manned by my own mother. Unbelievable."

"Is the service over?" I asked Nancy.

"Nah. But I couldn't stay in there any longer. I think you guys had the right idea. This is all the service Jenna would've wanted."

I winked at Amanda, who was nonchalantly dabbing at her eyes with the corner of her scarf. "To Jenna," she said quietly, "who as it turns out was actually the one who was really sick and probably knew it all along, but let me throw my tantrums anyway."

Nancy put her arm around Amanda as she took a sip from her glass and then threw the remainder into the lake, glass and all.

We laughed so hard we almost ended up in a dogpile right there on the dead grass.

Amanda looked immensely satisfied. "I always wanted to do that."

Chapter 30

The sun was sinking low when Dad came out to the lake to retrieve me. I said goodbye to Amanda first, then Owen, then Nancy. I tried not to cry, but when I thought about how I might not see the Walkers much now since there was no Jenna to visit, I couldn't help it.

"It's okay, love," Nancy murmured as she kissed the top of my head. "And believe me, you haven't seen the last of us." She looked into my face, flicked her eyes over to Owen, and winked at me. I smiled, and Nancy reached into her pocket. "Oh—I almost forgot. This is for you, from Jenna." She placed a glittering blue pen into my hand.

Tears instantly materialized, and I inspected my new treasure through blurred eyes.

"She loved this pen," Nancy said softly as I gazed at the exquisite hibiscus flower painted onto the cap. "She wanted you to have it because she loved you, too."

I nodded, not trusting myself to speak, and gave her hand one more squeeze before turning to go.

"Thank you, Jenna," I whispered into the wind.

When Dad and I arrived home the house was empty and quiet, except for Mom sitting on the couch, poring over an old photo album.

She paused when we came in. "How was the service?" she asked quietly.

I smiled. "It was…sweet."

Mom smiled a sad smile, patting the couch cushion next to her. "Sit?" As if after I did that, everything else would be easy.

I walked over to the couch and Dad followed, and I soon found myself to be the center of a parent sandwich. I was too numb to do anything but attempt to memorize the cover of the magazine resting on the coffee table.

"I've been sitting here looking at all these old pictures."

I glanced over and recognized a picture of Mom with her hair in a tight perm like she used to wear it, and those glasses! "Nice look, Mom." I glanced at her and noticed a tiny smirk.

She turned the page, and I saw a few pictures from when Daniel was a toddler, bundled in my mom's arms while she beamed at the camera. Behind her shoulder, a timid Annie gazed up.

Another page, another picture: Daniel in his Little

League uniform and Mom right beside him, radiant with pride. Me—maybe eight years old—a short distance apart sitting on a blanket, gazing at them.

"It's not fun to feel like the forgotten kid," Mom said softly. "I've been looking through these photos and home movies and watching how we showed off Daniel, and Tracy was this hyperactive, happy kid and nothing seemed to bother her. And you were this teeny, quiet thing. I think these past couple of months you probably felt like you were getting lost in the shuffle all over again. I'm sorry."

Dad squeezed my shoulder.

I didn't know what to say. I'd waited all my life for them to admit I had a point about all this invisible middle child stuff. I guess I spent so much time thinking about the actual problem that I never figured out what would happen if someone tried to fix it. I *did* know I didn't want my parents to beat themselves up over it, but what did I want them to do instead?

Dad reached over to the side table for an envelope. "And there's this." He handed it over to me, already opened. Inside I found a typed copy of my writing prompt from that day in English class, and a letter.

My eyes skimmed the letter and I felt my eyebrows lift. "An honorable mention—wow!"

Mom laughed. "Since when are you over here entering writing contests? We think they should've given you first place." She and Dad beamed proudly at me, and I wished I could freeze the moment forever.

Dad spoke up. "It was so sad, reading it. We want you to know you're not invisible. You're not unimportant. Even though things have been so different lately, we see you."

I felt my whole face crumple, and the tears fell down, hot. "I should've tried to pitch in and understand a little better what you guys were going through," I said, not meeting anyone's eyes. "But I was just...hurt. It's been hard."

"I know," Mom said. "It's been so unbelievably tough on us all."

There was a heavy silence, but a ray of peace filtered through it. Maybe it was enough for now that they knew how I felt, and we could all try to be more understanding. But still the question remained: Why did any of this have to happen in the first place?

I took a deep breath. "I've felt lonely and been scared about what would happen to our family, and I still don't know why God would allow this to happen to all of us. What did we do?"

"Oh Annie, this wasn't a punishment," Mom said.

"No, it wasn't a punishment at all," Dad echoed. "Things like this are just part of our world. But look at how much worse it could've been. Daniel survived two surgeries, the tumor is gone, he's able to speak and walk around, and our little family is still intact. It's an amazing thing. I know it's hard to see this now, but God has blessed us even through this difficult situation."

It was quiet for a little while as I took this in. I guess

I hadn't thought of it that way—that we'd been protected from things being even worse. I mean, just look what Jenna's family was going through! All things considered, I guess you could call our family's survival a blessing.

Mom seemed to read my thoughts. "I'm sorry for not understanding about Nancy, Jenna, and Owen. I can see why you wanted to spend time with other people who could help, and I'm glad they could be there for you. I'm so very sorry Jenna is gone."

Hearing Jenna's name broke something loose inside of me, and I felt a pressure so sharp and deep in my chest that it seemed like my heart might stop beating altogether. "I still can't believe Jenna's just *gone*," I whispered as the tears began to fall. "There are so many things I would've told her. I never realized before how many invisible things make up a person, and they're gone. Everything about her has disappeared and all that's left is this hole where she used to be." I held up the hibiscus pen. "And also, I have this pen. I have a hole in my heart, and this pen."

Tentatively, Mom reached out to take me in her arms, and the barrier broke. There were hurts and there were misunderstandings between us that ran so deep. This wall hadn't been built in a day, and I knew it would take more than one night to demolish it. Still, it felt wonderful to be taking the first sledgehammer blows to destroy it, together.

Dad put a warm hand on my back.

"Thanks for coming to my recital," I whispered as Mom held me tighter.

I could practically hear her smiling.

"Always, Annie."

I retired to my room, my body more drained than I could ever remember feeling. My heart felt like a pinwheel of emotions that someone had set into a huge gust of wind so I felt everything all at once. There was still a profound sadness underneath it all. But there was something else… something deeper. A feeling that something had clicked into place.

I sat on my bed and reached out to pet Smokey, and thought about how even with everything so messy right now, there were some things I just knew.

I knew Rachel would continue to be a wonderful friend who would always try to understand, that Tracy would forever be the big sister to look out for me, and even Daniel could be my friend. But I would never have another Jenna. She was special beyond replacing, and that's the way it had to stay.

I knew a year from today Nancy, Owen, Amanda, and I would find a way to meet at the lake next to the hospital. We would laugh and cry and drink our disgusting sugary tea while telling the stories to keep Jenna's memory alive. And Owen would know I was here, when he was ready, and when neither of us had any more jet black in our eyes.

I knew God answered my prayer asking for friends to turn into family in case mine fell apart. Because it did fall apart for a little while, and He sent the Walkers to take care of me. First Jenna rescued me, then she left me Owen and Nancy to make sure I'd always be okay. And now that my family was being sewn back together I would still have them, and I had Rachel, and Travis, and I had a church family, too.

I knew life would likely always be a struggle for Daniel—at least, life would be different than before. I guess we'd all suffered, all hurt, all changed dramatically, but Daniel was the only one who wore his scar on the outside.

I knew our family might feel at times like strangers thrown together, with mismatched dreams conflicting—sticking out awkwardly like so many odd ingredients thrown into a pot. And God was up there seasoning and stirring everything together, knowing the plan and that something beautiful would come of it all.

Jenna was right. Everything would be okay. There was more love out there in the world than I thought—I wasn't ever alone. There was such a wide circle all around me, filled with brilliant, golden light.

A Final Note

Serious illness brings so many difficulties into a family's life, and I believe faith in God and the support of our friends and family is what helped carry mine through. I know we were lucky. I thank God for the patience and wisdom of friends whose support and understanding echo still, and for the strength of my family to remain dedicated to healing.

I'm so proud to tell you that my "little" brother grew up, unfailing in his faith, optimism, and the deep conviction that he is not broken. After physical therapy and surgeries to loosen tendons in his hand and foot, he regained some motor function and lost much of his limp. He has taught himself how to work around the limitations he still has, and worked hard to achieve a career in the healthcare field. He often gets to encourage those who have had experiences just like his, telling them "Here's how I overcame it, and you can, too!"

For more information about brain tumors in children, visit the Pediatric Brain Tumor Foundation website (www.pbtfus.org). Another great resource on brain tumors and how you can help make a difference is the National Brain Tumor Society (www.braintumor.org).

If you are the sibling of a child with special needs, I'm happy to recommend the sibling support groups offered by Family Resource Associates (www.frainc.org); the Sibling Support Project offered by Kindering (www.kindering.org); and SuperSibs, a program offered through Alex's Lemonade Stand (www.alexslemonade.org).